The Christmas House

Elizabeth Bromke

Cover design by Jessica Parker

THE CHRISTMAS HOUSE
PUBLISHING IN THE PINES
White Mountains, Arizona

For Aunt Margaret and Grandma Engelhard, best friends.

Chapter 1: 2013

An icy, wintery wind curled around Fern Monroe and deposited her like an errant snowflake through the front door of the Dotson Museum.

She rarely left work during lunchtime but had forgotten her tote at home. After a brisk walk to the sandwich shop down the street, Fern returned, a brown sack clutched beneath her berry-red nails.

Few visitors milled about inside the foyer, and Fern was glad of that. Though she was fine to answer questions and play docent when necessary, her introversion felt heavy that day.

Ideally, the thirty-something curator with fur-lined snow boots and a sturdy winter coat (a QVC clearance purchase) would disappear into her little office space and get back to her job as she munched away on a plain turkey sandwich.

But despite the routine work that awaited Fern Monroe, fate had different plans on that frosty December afternoon.

Sitting squarely in the center of Fern's desk between the computer and a towering stack of reference books was her task of the day. A possible movie prop from the film *Seabiscuit.*

As she turned the heavy piece over in her hand, Fern booted up the PC.

According to her boss, a donor had dropped it off the afternoon before, claiming it was a genuine horse bit from the set.

The Dotson didn't typically display movie props—and especially not *modern* movie props—but it was Fern's job to verify the authenticity of donated items.

She took a sip from her to-go cup of hot cocoa and browsed the web for a local film expert.

After jotting down some leads, Fern stumbled across a hokey-looking chat room: Louisville Movie Buffs.

Curious, Fern created a quick profile and joined.

***

MiracleOnPineTreeLn has entered the chat.

GoneWithTheGale is typing...

GoneWithTheGale: Welcome to Louisville Movie Buffs! I'm Stedman, the unofficial chat moderator.

MiracleOnPineTreeLn is typing...

MiracleOnPineTreeLn: Hello, Stedman. My name is Fern.

GoneWithTheGale: How did you find us, Fern?

MiracleOnPineTreeLn: Dumb luck, I suppose.

MiracleOnPineTreeLn is typing...

MiracleOnPineTreeLn: I work at the Dotson Museum. Research brought me here. You folks don't happen to know anything about the movie *Seabiscuit*, do you? I suppose I fell down the rabbit hole. Anyway, I love movies, so I figured I'd join even if you can't help me.

GoneWithTheGale: Unfortunately, racing movies are not my forte. Classics are. And, I have to admit that I'm the only one who uses this chat room, other than my cousin, Shari, and my friend, Tim. We jump on to chat to each other sometimes, but mostly this place is as dead as a door nail. Honestly, I don't even know why I'm in here right now...

MiracleOnPineTreeLn: I thought chat rooms were ancient. But, I did enjoy coming up with a screen name. How nostalgic. Took me back to my college days.

GoneWithTheGale: I'm glad you joined! It looks like you got the memo on our handles, huh?

MiracleOnPineTreeLn is typing...

MiracleOnPineTreeLn: ???

GoneWithTheGale: Your screen name/handle is a movie pun or a play on a movie title. Is that your street? Pine Tree Lane?

MiracleOnPineTreeLn is typing...

MiracleOnPineTreeLn: I can neither confirm nor deny. You're a stranger!

GoneWithTheGale: We can fix that. **Hi, Fern. I'm Stedman Gale. Marketing consultant, one of six children, and UofL alumnus, class of 2002. I'm thirty-nine years old, six foot one, in good shape, and—much to my mother's dismay—I'm single. There, now we aren't strangers anymore ;)

MiracleOnPineTreeLn: You sound like a catch.

GoneWithTheGale: Now, Fern, this chat room was not founded under pretenses. If you want a hook-up, you'll have to look elsewhere.

MiracleOnPineTreeLn is typing...

GoneWithTheGale: I'm just kidding, Fern!

MiracleOnPineTreeLn is typing...

GoneWithTheGale: But I *am* single...

MiracleOnPineTreeLn: Well, Stedman Gale, I have no romantic notions about a wacky movie nut from the web. But while we're at it... My name is Fern Monroe. I'm forty-one years old, petite, blonde-haired and blue-eyed.

GoneWithTheGale: You sound like a catch.

MiracleOnPineTreeLn: My mother would agree with you.

GoneWithTheGale: Is she, too, dismayed that you're single?

MiracleOnPineTreeLn is typing...

GoneWithTheGale: *Are* you single?

MiracleOnPineTreeLn: Now, Stedman, this chat room was not founded under pretenses. If you want a hook-up, you'll have to look elsewhere.

GoneWithTheGale: What if I want more than a hook-up?

MiracleOnPineTreeLn is typing...

GoneWithTheGale: Maybe I'll change my handle to *GoneTooFar*. Sometimes I talk too much. Or write too much, as the case may be.

MiracleOnPineTreeLn: Are you looking for a soul mate?

GoneWithTheGale: I think it's safe to say that if a man's favorite movie stars Clark Gable and Vivien Leigh, well then—he's looking for his soul mate.

MiracleOnPineTreeLn is typing...

MiracleOnPineTreeLn: Hm...

GoneWithTheGale: That's all I get? A "hm?" I'm spilling my heart, and you, a veritable stranger, can only write "hm?"

MiracleOnPineTreeLn: Hah. I'm sorry, Stedman. It was a good "hm."

GoneWithTheGale: Oh, well. I think we can work with that, then.

MiracleOnPineTreeLn: I hate to leave, but I have to get back to work.

MiracleOnPineTreeLn is typing...

GoneWithTheGale: I understand!

MiracleOnPineTreeLn is typing...

GoneWithTheGale: It's been nice talking with you, MiracleOnPineTreeLn.

MiracleOnPineTreeLn: Stedman, wait.

GoneWithTheGale: I'm not going anywhere...

MiracleOnPineTreeLn: This was fun!

GoneWithTheGale: I agree :)

MiracleOnPineTreeLn: I'll be back online later tonight... say around six?

GoneWithTheGale: You've got a date.

Chapter 2: Present Day

Clad in a brand new, pine green sweater with mistletoe earrings dangling from below her blonde up do, Fern Gale clutched a serving tray. At the center of the tray, a few errant clumps of leftover white meat lay limp.

Overhead, radio speakers transitioned from "Jingle Bells" to "Holy Night." The crowd thinned out and the low murmur of jolly eaters was reduced to a few stragglers and the remaining volunteers.

Fern shifted the tray in her hands. Indecision clouded her judgment—either spoon the little bit of turkey into a Tupperware from the kitchen and be on her merry way, or trash it as if she were the Grinch. A forty-five-year-old, female Grinch.

Of course she should save it. What was the point of serving the less fortunate if you were going to dump the leftover food? Didn't that undermine the whole idea of *doing good*?

Nodding to herself, Fern lifted a brown boot and started for the kitchen.

"Oh, Fern, here. I'll scrape that for you." Liesl Hart pried the tray from Fern's grip and bounced to the nearest trash bin. She stopped short, clicking her tongue at the height of the waste, then set the tray down and proceeded to lift her foot over top of the teetering pile of soda pop cans, greasy napkins, and soiled paper plates. At last, she jumped up and *into* the darn thing.

Fern rushed in behind her. "Liesl, let me help, for goodness sake."

Laughter took hold of both of them, and Fern laced her fingers through Liesl's, helping the woman to jounce up and down until the trash had sufficiently compacted to allow Liesl to scrape the few leftovers on top.

Liesl's hands were smooth and clean. Her nails carefully painted brick red. Short. Squared off. Functional but pretty. She was both masculine and feminine. The duality was quite beautiful, and Fern felt important helping to steady this woman.

As Liesl descended, Fern caught a whiff of floral shampoo. It reminded her of her mom. Eleanor Monroe always smelled like shampoo. Fern clutched briefly at her chest just as Liesl landed back on the rec hall floor.

"There. Whew!" Liesl clapped her hands and moved on to do the same with cranberry sauce dregs and leftover potatoes.

Fern suppressed an urge to cry out, This is for the homeless! Shouldn't we save the leftovers and dole them back out tomorrow?

Or, at the very least, maybe the volunteers could divide the remains and tote them home? Turkey sandwiches for a week—wasn't that the post-Thanksgiving tradition of any true, red-blooded American?

Then again, who was Fern to judge? She, herself, followed few conventions of society, really. Accepting instead a quiet, lonely life.

She *preferred* to stay in. She *preferred* to keep social interactions for only the most important of occasions. Fern wasn't one to waste energy and makeup on any old weekend night. She saved all of that for special events. Like holidays.

Fern loved holidays. Even Halloween when there was no charity dinner where she could turn up and help. Still she loved it. She loved watching Alfred Hitchcock films for a week straight.

And she loved carving a pumpkin with grand plans to roast and salt the seeds soon thereafter. Of course, Fern typically didn't get around to roasting the seeds. Hauling the rotting pumpkin to the garbage hopper was as much follow-through as she could muster.

But she mostly loved the sweeter holidays, looking especially forward to Little Flock's Community Thanksgiving. A sweeping title for what was simply the Little Flock Catholic Parish's charity meal.

Fern had begun volunteering the year after her mother passed because she knew it was her duty to fill that role and because it was a chance to chat with the locals; many of whom she'd simply never connected with throughout her life.

Plus, it always felt good. Rubbing elbows with Hickory Grove high society like Liesl Hart gave Fern a bit of a thrill and even inspired her.

Maybe *today* would be the day she'd deep clean her house. Maybe *today* would be the day she'd book a trip to the salon. Maybe *today* would be the day she'd get back to being her old self. The Fern who everyone saw as a mysterious beauty. The Fern who, though somewhat isolated, was happy and pleasant and *normal.*

The clean-up was complete. No more picked-over food left. The long, narrow, folding tables had been neatly stacked against the far wall. Warming trays and food storage tubs had been soaked and scrubbed and were now drying along the

Formica counter that stretched out from a utilitarian, stainless steel sink.

Liesl had scuttled away with a few other women from the Ladies Auxiliary. Each likely heading to her very own Thanksgiving dinner. Or maybe to the Thanksgiving dinners that their families were hosting—bustling dinners with men shouting at television screens as other men, uniformed and sweating, stood on a green field with hands on hips.

In these scenes, Fern could picture children squabbling over toys, or perhaps *devices*.

She could picture elegant tablescapes with mixed textures and gleaming candles, somehow safe from the hectic flow of traffic. Cousins and aunts and uncles wondering through fire-warmed homes, bored and plump with turkey. Rowdy affairs, to be sure.

Fern smiled wanly at Anthony, the only other volunteer left.

"Thanks for helping today, Fern," he said as they walked out together. He held the door for her and she passed through, awkwardly waiting as he fumbled to lock the building.

Those who needed shelter for the night would be back in a few hours. A different volunteer would arrive by then. The chain effect of charity was strong in Hickory Grove. Fern knew this.

"Oh, it was my pleasure, Anthony. Really. What a nice event." She looked off across the cemetery that sprawled up the little hill beyond the church buildings.

Anthony hesitated, offering Fern a tight-lipped smile. "I've got to get home. You know Jackie," he added, squinting into the late afternoon sun.

Fern did not know Jackie, really. She knew *of* her, as her mother would always trill—her voice perched high in her throat as though Eleanor Monroe had heard of such people but was too busy to *know* such people.

Was Jackie an overbearing wife? Was she demanding and severe? Did she kiss her husband hello and goodbye perfunctorily or did she kiss him with urgency? Desperate for him to never leave her? Desperate for him to return home?

"Enjoy your supper," Fern offered, smiling as she turned toward her own vehicle.

It was early yet. She had hours to fill before it was time to gear up for Black Friday. Empty hours where she would feel the pull of loneliness. The uncomfortable absence of people. Of noise. No one to irritate her or remind her why she *chose* to live alone and stay inside that loneliness with such dedication.

Chapter 3: 2013

GoneWithTheGale has entered the chat.

MiracleOnPineTreeLn: Good evening :)

GoneWithTheGale: Hi, Fern!

MiracleOnPineTreeLn: How was your day?

GoneWithTheGale: Great, actually. It's funny—when you start your morning by talking to a beautiful woman, your day is automatically terrific. No matter what happens!

MiracleOnPineTreeLn: You have no idea whether I'm beautiful...

GoneWithTheGale: You write beautifully. And, what can I say? I'm a sucker for blonde-haired, blue-eyed women with the last name Monroe.

MiracleOnPineTreeLn: Hah. I'm no Marilyn.

GoneWithTheGale: And I'm no Clark Gable.

MiracleOnPineTreeLn: In that case, I'd better go...

GoneWithTheGale: Hey, now!

MiracleOnPineTreeLn: Just kidding ;)

GoneWithTheGale: Fern?

MiracleOnPineTreeLn: Yes...?

GoneWithTheGale: You never answered my question.

MiracleOnPineTreeLn: Which one?

GoneWithTheGale: Are you single?

MiracleOnPineTreeLn: I'm a couple years older than you.

GoneWithTheGale: That wasn't my question.

MiracleOnPineTreeLn: Okay, well. My best friend is my mother...

GoneWithTheGale: Hm. Did you lie to me?

MiracleOnPineTreeLn: About what?

GoneWithTheGale: Are you sure you're a blonde woman and not a dark-haired motel owner by the last name of Bates?

MiracleOnPineTreeLn: You like Hitchcock, too?

GoneWithTheGale: You're avoiding all my questions now.

MiracleOnPineTreeLn: I am a blonde woman. And yes.

GoneWithTheGale: Yes?

MiracleOnPineTreeLn: Yes, I'm single. All right? There. I've said it.

GoneWithTheGale: So what have you been doing for the last forty-one years?

MiracleOnPineTreeLn: What do you mean?

GoneWithTheGale: You work at Dotson. You love movies, especially classics. Ever married?

MiracleOnPineTreeLn: Never, actually. You?

GoneWithTheGale: Almost. Came close.

MiracleOnPineTreeLn: What happened?

MiracleOnPineTreeLn: If you don't mind my asking...

GoneWithTheGale: Not at all. I'm a homebody. She wasn't. Don't get me wrong. I enjoy going out for drinks. And to the movies, obviously. I travel a lot for work, and it's exhausting. So, when I'm home, I just want to be home. She was opposite. A social butterfly, always on the move.

MiracleOnPineTreeLn: I'm similar.

GoneWithTheGale: You like to go out a lot?

MiracleOnPineTreeLn: No, I mean I'm similar to you. A homebody.

GoneWithTheGale: Hey, is that you?

MiracleOnPineTreeLn: Is what me?

GoneWithTheGale: You changed your profile photo on the page.

MiracleOnPineTreeLn is typing...

GoneWithTheGale: You're right—you're no Marilyn.

MiracleOnPineTreeLn is typing...

GoneWithTheGale: You blow her out of the water.

MiracleOnPineTreeLn: Well, that's ridiculous.

GoneWithTheGale: If you look like your photo, then it's true. You're beautiful.

MiracleOnPineTreeLn: It's a flattering picture. I admit.

GoneWithTheGale: I probably don't own a flattering picture of myself. Here's a recent one, though.

MiracleOnPineTreeLn: I just got your attachment. You have kind eyes, Stedman. It's a nice photo. You're handsome.

GoneWithTheGale: Aw, shucks. Thanks :)

MiracleOnPineTreeLn: I've never done this before.

GoneWithTheGale: Exchanged photos with a man online?

MiracleOnPineTreeLn: Exactly.

GoneWithTheGale: Why didn't you ever get married, Fern?

MiracleOnPineTreeLn is typing...

MiracleOnPineTreeLn: I'm not sure. I've always liked the idea. Just never found *the one*, I guess.

GoneWithTheGale: Any serious relationships?

MiracleOnPineTreeLn: No. A few dates over the years. I guess that's what happens when you're a homebody. A little weird, huh?

GoneWithTheGale: I don't think so.

MiracleOnPineTreeLn: If I'm not careful, I'm going to turn into a cat lady.

GoneWithTheGale: Do you have lots of cats?

MiracleOnPineTreeLn: No. None, actually.

GoneWithTheGale: Don't go buying any!

MiracleOnPineTreeLn: I won't. My apartment won't allow it. Anyway, I'm looking to move back to Hickory Grove.

GoneWithTheGale: Is that where you're from?

MiracleOnPineTreeLn: Yes. Heard of it?

GoneWithTheGale: Nope. Is it a suburb?

MiracleOnPineTreeLn: No. It's a small town just north of the Ohio.

GoneWithTheGale: Oh, so you're a Yankee.

MiracleOnPineTreeLn: Hah. As much of a Yankee as one can be when you grow up in a small farming town on the river.

GoneWithTheGale: Why do you want to move back?

MiracleOnPineTreeLn: My father passed a couple years ago.

GoneWithTheGale: I'm so sorry to hear that.

MiracleOnPineTreeLn: Oh, thank you. It's fine. But my mother has become lonely. She doesn't have any family left, and since I'm not the sort who *needs* to be in a big city, I decided to go home.

GoneWithTheGale: Are you going to live with her?

MiracleOnPineTreeLn: I'm not sure. Probably. Our house is big. There's enough space. I should live there.

GoneWithTheGale: I would, if I were you.

MiracleOnPineTreeLn: You would what?

GoneWithTheGale: I would live with my mom. If she were alone and I were alone and if we had a big house out in the country. It sounds idyllic.

MiracleOnPineTreeLn: Stedman, we should do this every day.

GoneWithTheGale: Do what?

MiracleOnPineTreeLn: Chat. I like talking to you.

GoneWithTheGale: Okay. Let's do it every day.

GoneWithTheGale: Chat, I mean ;)

MiracleOnPineTreeLn: I knew what you meant.

GoneWithTheGale: I knew you would.

Chapter 4

Once she pulled into her driveway, the sadness dissipated a little. Toffee would be waiting for her Thanksgiving dinner, and Fern was looking forward to their nightly routine.

Peering over the steering wheel, she rolled up the long drive onto her property and then into the garage. The tennis ball finally made contact with her windshield, assuring her she was home. Safe and alone. Alone but safe.

Unable to swallow the lump that had formed in her throat, she spied her pretty little Persian cat prancing up the hall, pleased that Fern had returned. Fern tickled Toffee behind the ears and promised her dinner was coming soon.

After producing a small can of wet cat food, Fern raised the heat on the thermostat. It was late November, and Hickory Grove had been slow to accept winter weather. But it was here now, and the forecast reported a looming snowstorm.

Fern tried to keep her utility bills down, but she tended to prefer a warm house. To compensate, she dropped the thermostat when she was gone and raised it only when she returned.

Her husband had always admonished that it was better to regulate the inside temperature. Avoid the extremes. But that was when he was around to bring to life a roaring fire in their small apartment in Louisville. It worked there. Heating her childhood home, a veritable manor, was another matter. And while Fern loved a crackling fire, she wasn't as good at keeping it alive.

As the furnace thrummed to life, Fern headed upstairs, stopping first in her dressing room, where she rehung her new blouse and neatly folded her slacks and shelved them.

Then, she moved to the bathroom and stripped out of her undergarments, hanging her red brassiere on the doorknob as usual. It was something of a bad habit—hanging her bra on the doorknob—and one that had irritated both her mother and, later, her husband.

Why she even *owned* a red bra was a fluke. An impulsive, late-night QVC order. But she wore it for special events because, ironically, it laid nicely and discreetly beneath a silk blouse. Red was the only color in stock, and Fern liked having a small personal secret when she was in public. It emboldened her.

Though the water was still cool, she stepped inside and the tears came at last. She cried out of self-pity, mostly. Grief, too. Loneliness, by and large.

By the time the water had warmed up, she wasn't crying anymore. Or, if she was, she couldn't tell. The hot water on the back of her neck massaged the sobs away. Still, her head had begun to ache.

Fern forced herself to stretch the shower as long as she could, massaging shampoo into her long, straw-colored hair before adding a palmful of cream rinse and working it up the shaft and into her dull roots.

She hadn't cut her hair since she'd last colored her roots. It was a few inches too long and the ends were dried out. A shampoo and rinse would do nothing to mitigate its limp, lifeless, shape. But, it would smell good.

The water turned cool, completing its cycle through the water heater, apparently. Since Fern was no martyr, she quickly rinsed herself off and stepped out and into the robe her mother had bought her for her forty-first birthday. Fern remembered the birthday, because she would meet Stedman the very next day. Or, at least, she would have her first "chat" with him. She hated to associate a special gift from her late mother with *Stedman Gale*.

After rubbing night cream into her face, hand cream into her hands, and changing into a flannel nightgown, Fern popped a couple of aspirins and set a kettle to boil milk. It wasn't even five o'clock, and Fern had no leftover turkey to nibble on. But she had her cocoa powder and marshmallows, and she had microwavable bags of popcorn. All that was left was to get everything situated onto her TV tray and post up in the coziest place in her house: the great room sofa.

Christmas movies were well underway on all of Fern's favorite channels, but still she opted to start with a football game. This way, she could browse the web on her laptop and remove herself from any and every bit of holiday blues.

Then, once she'd bored herself to death over sports jargon and set up no fewer than ten browser tabs with Black Friday tips for success, she could maybe—just maybe—sneak over to Hallmark or Lifetime and tune into something her mother would have loved. Or even Turner Classic Movies. *It's a Wonderful Life* was sure to be airing soon.

Fern thought of the river boat. Their first date.

Maybe she'd stay away from the classics this year.

Maybe not.

***

Four hours, three mugs of hot cocoa, and one bag of popcorn later, Fern awoke with a start. She'd likely fallen asleep to *Jingle Bells and Cinnamon*, a made-for-TV movie which was long over. Commercials sang out from the screen and across the room, rousing her from a too-late nap. Toffee snored at her feet.

Fern wiped her mouth with the back of her hand and shifted her weight across the sinking sofa cushions. She began to pull the afghan back up over her shoulders. She could tune the commercials out, after all. Fern always slept with the television on. It kept her from nightmares. Grounded her in a fantasy of laundry detergent jingles and Diet Coke promises.

But then, just as she sank deeper into the back corner of Eleanor's floral patterned couch (purchased at a furniture liquidation sale in the early nineties), she realized she'd almost forgotten.

It was Monroe Family Tradition. Christmas decorations went up the very night of Thanksgiving. Every year. Without fail.

Fern had adjusted the tradition only slightly, in fact. After Eleanor died, Fern stopped taking the decorations down at all.

There was little to be said of the matter.

And so Fern said nothing about it.

She said nothing about it when people began to ask her at church. She said nothing when they inquired if she needed a little help as she was checking out at the corner market. She said nothing when well-meaning church ladies whispered to her after the service, offering to send their husbands over in the afternoon with a ladder and a storage box.

So, nowadays, in order to uphold the Monroe Family Tradition, all she had to do on Thanksgiving evening was to turn on the lights. Of course, quite a many of the bulbs burnt out long ago. In fact, if Fern had ever dared to move past her veranda and out to the street one evening, she'd learn that the lights, when on, looked more like a handful of lightning bugs had been caught in spiderwebs and just hung there, sort of buzzing on and off.

But Fern never went out at night, so she didn't know that. She just hoped they were enough—enough for the memory of her mom.

Slipping out from the blanket, careful not to disturb Toffee, Fern padded out of the great room and to the foyer, where a lineup of light switches stood at ease. She flipped the one in question, and the windows that framed the door glowed anew. Fern trudged back to the sofa and found Toffee in her spot. She lifted the pillow of a feline and snuggled her close to her chest as she lay down and willed herself back to sleep.

The next morning, the first morning of the Christmas season, Fern felt better. More capable. Though many things about the holidays had become painful since her mother's passing, Fern had found a new outlet for her Christmas heartache.

Bargain shopping.

Chapter 5: 2013

MiracleOnPineTreeLn has entered the chat.

GoneWithTheGale is typing...

GoneWithTheGale: Good morning, beautiful!

MiracleOnPineTreeLn: Good morning... handsome ;)

GoneWithTheGale: Fern, I miss you.

MiracleOnPineTreeLn: What do you mean? We chatted until midnight. Remember?

GoneWithTheGale: No, I mean I *miss* you.

MiracleOnPineTreeLn: Stedman, how can you miss someone you haven't even met?

GoneWithTheGale: I dunno. Maybe we're soul mates.

MiracleOnPineTreeLn: Soul mates? Because we both love classic movies? I'm sure you could find other women who like movies. Women with more to give you than me. Big-city women who go out and have fun.

GoneWithTheGale: We've been over this, Fern. No. I don't want to go out and have fun.

MiracleOnPineTreeLn: Hah. Gee, thanks!

GoneWithTheGale: Fern, seriously. You're beautiful and smart. You're interesting. I mean it. Anyways, you know I'd rather stay in to watch movies and talk.

MiracleOnPineTreeLn is typing...

GoneWithTheGale: I know you agree with me, because *you* are *my* soul mate. Fern, believe me when I say I miss you. I missed you before I knew you. I miss you today. I always will. Even if we never meet, I'll miss you.

MiracleOnPineTreeLn: You don't think we'll meet?

GoneWithTheGale: I hope we do...

MiracleOnPineTreeLn: Then let's do it.

MiracleOnPineTreeLn: Meet, I mean...

GoneWithTheGale: Yes! Let's do it. Did you know *It's a Wonderful Life* is playing at the river boat casino?

MiracleOnPineTreeLn: Oh, that's right! The original!

GoneWithTheGale: I'd love to take you. Are you free tonight?

MiracleOnPineTreeLn is typing...

GoneWithTheGale: Or tomorrow?

MiracleOnPineTreeLn is typing...

GoneWithTheGale: ...Hey, this was *your* idea...

MiracleOnPineTreeLn: Isn't it a little early for Christmas movies?

GoneWithTheGale: It's September, Fern! Where's your holiday spirit? If the river boat casino says it's time to watch Christmas movies, then it's time to watch Christmas movies.

MiracleOnPineTreeLn: Well, I do love Christmas.

GoneWithTheGale: And I love movies.

MiracleOnPineTreeLn: Me, too. And I love... I love talking to you, Stedman. Or writing to you. Chatting. Whatever this is...

GoneWithTheGale is typing...

GoneWithTheGale: I love talking to you, too, Fern Monroe. And I love writing to you and chatting with you. *Whatever this is.*

GoneWithTheGale: So what do you think? Dinner and drinks... James Stewart and Donna Reed... What more could a soul mate want?

MiracleOnPineTreeLn is typing...

GoneWithTheGale: You know, Fern, if we meet, then you'll believe me.

MiracleOnPineTreeLn: Believe you?

GoneWithTheGale: You'll believe me the next time I say I miss you.

Chapter 6

Black Friday was crucial to Fern's mental health.

Fortunately, she was close enough to head into Louisville if she needed to hit up the usual big box stores for extras. But the small shops around Hickory Grove had learned to jump on the consumerist bandwagon. She'd poke and hunt through second-hand stores and quilt shops until she alighted upon rare and interesting pieces at steep markdowns.

Eventually, Fern intended to open an online shop and sell all the treasures she'd collected over the years. She had an eye for value; she knew she did. However, she didn't trust other people to understand real collectibles. Brokering for an antiques auction website had taught her that.

So, she saved up everything she found for the one day when she would feel inspired and motivated enough to take the plunge and open her own business, rather than work for snooty antique elites who'd send pointed emails and passive-aggressively suggest how she mismanaged the deals between the sellers and the buyers. As though Fern hadn't worked in a museum for years. As if she didn't have two degrees and a brain. These fools who sat behind the computer screen in their high-rise offices in New York and Los Angeles and depended on the internet to make them money.

Of course, Fern had not always begrudged technology its place in the world. For being the sort of person who preferred things of the past to things of the present, she'd found early on how useful technology was in the study of the world around, even the old world.

And, notably, technology was how she met her husband.

Back in 2013, and just before salacious dating apps had taken the world by storm, she met Stedman in a good, old-fashioned chat room. *Louisville Movie Buffs*.

Fern loved to watch movies with her mom. Any and all. Their inside jokes often revolved around cheesy seventies flicks or melodramatic classics.

Stedman was a true film expert, it turned out. He'd studied film a little as he was earning his business degree. He thought, she supposed, that taking a position in marketing would be parallel to actually working a movie. Fern never saw the connection. All she saw was that he was hapless sort of guy who ended up traveling for work more often than not.

And, if she was honest, that never bothered her much.

Until Eleanor died, of course.

***

It was just after four in the afternoon when Fern finished the last of her expedition.

She ended up filling her trunk with Louisville treasures this year. Once she'd driven by the local options, she noted that—surprisingly—there was no window art in any of the little boutiques in Hickory Grove. Nothing screaming that whatever she could find inside she could leave with five of them and for almost free. Nothing that promised a good, old fashioned deal. So she'd moved on to Louisville through the pre-dawn traffic in the frigid air that whipped up around the cars while they drove along the Ohio River.

Now, as Fern pulled back down Pine Tree Lane to the tune of "Silent Night" spilling from her stereo, it occurred to her that it had been snowing for nearly her entire drive. The first snow of the season. As predicted by the weatherman.

A wintry fortune, indeed and she was almost too distracted to notice.

Eleanor had loved the snow. Fern did, too.

Now, she maneuvered into a three-point turn in order to back up her long driveway, and the white flakes began to fall more heavily.

She advanced the speed on the wipers but realized that wouldn't help her see through the back windshield. Muttering under her breath, Fern carefully crunched back over fresh snow and toward where the garage door would be. Unable to see enough to confidently go any farther, she put the car in park and jabbed off the beginning of a Dean Martin song.

She had enough forethought to back in for unloading, but now she was faced with the inconvenience of walking through snow in her clogs.

With a heavy sigh, Fern popped the button on the garage remote and waited just long enough that she could dash up the rest of the drive and beneath the yawning door.

Once inside, she propped her hands on her hips and studied the distance of the car from the garage. It was too great and the afternoon conditions too snowy for her to even bother with unloading and sorting.

It was just as well. Christmas movies were surely in full force, and she was dog-tired. The only real option was a shower, hot cocoa, popcorn, and her television set.

Monday would arrive soon enough. She'd better take full advantage of her free time in order to drink in the start to the holiday season.

But as soon as Fern began to turn away from the snowy scene out among her expansive property, four human forms, clad from head to toe in puffy snow gear, trudged through the pelting snowflakes and growing blanket of white, directly up her drive.

Fern hardly ever had visitors. With highly—*highly*—rare exceptions would someone ever choose to cross the invisible border from the normal, nice world of small-town Hickory Grove and descend into her overgrown and undergroomed front yard.

Such was not always the case at 313 Pine Tree Lane. When Eleanor was alive, the women hosted frequent guests. The Schwan's delivery man often lingered on the front stoop as he stared in wide-eyed wonder at the beautiful Eleanor Monroe and her equally entrancing daughter.

And the Ladies Auxiliary from church would come along since Eleanor offered her home as the meeting location for organizing that month's charitable event. Others, too. Back then, Eleanor and Fern were simply the mother and daughter without men in their lives. Descendants of the Tuell family and Monroe family—some of Hickory Grove's more prominent early settlers. Their reputation was solid.

Out of reverence for her mother, Fern had never taken down a single framed photograph since her passing. The walls were still lined with the images of her ancestors—both Monroe and Tuell—as they sneered from beneath thick bubbles of glass.

All those auxiliary ladies had tried for more visits once Eleanor was gone, but Fern couldn't handle their so-called sympathy. She couldn't carry the burden of their pity or the depth of their curiosity over what would become of Eleanor's only daughter and best friend.

The rest of the town got the hint rather quickly—either through the gossip of the Ladies Auxiliary or through Fern's growing mounds of crap as they spilled forth from the door and bolstered the windows and trickled up on either sides of the house like moss growing in the nooks and crannies of a never-moved rock.

So, then, who were these intruders?

Frozen in the frame of the garage door, Fern was immobile as the interlopers strode, heel-toe, heel-toe, like a veritable set of bigfoot nesting dolls, up her driveway.

She squinted through fast-falling chunks of snow to see a woman take shape. The three other smaller snowsuits could only belong to the woman, such as smaller people tend to *belong* to bigger people.

Fern had a good guess that it was the obnoxious neighbor and her litter of free-range children. She considered pretending she had no recognition of this motley crew but thought better of it and held up her hand in a sweet, southern wave.

"Fern! Ms. Monroe!" The woman's voice cried out. They were almost *in* the garage now. Fern's neck pinched in pain but she forced a smile.

The figures now formed a line in the blustery evening atmosphere. Three children, indeed. One very small. One awkward in shape and stance. The middle one, tubby and greasy-faced, held forth a paper plate with plastic piled high on top.

Fern looked to the mother, her smile breaking way as she offered a quiet hello. It was peculiar this woman was calling Fern "Ms. Monroe." They weren't too far apart in age. They both knew as much.

When Fern couldn't seem to do more than smile and stare, one of the children made an attempt at small-talk. "You're our neighbor."

Fern found herself suppressing a giggle, though she had no real cause to suppress it. She nodded at the lanky speaker and answered, "Yes. And you're mine."

Fern glanced toward the mother who now smiled broadly as she smeared wet snow up her forehead and into her yellowy hair.

The littlest snowsuit began to whine, and as her mother reached to comfort her, the pudgy middle child interjected, "We baked you Christmas cookies." He (or she—it was unclear) thrust the plate across the threshold of the garage and Fern took note of the accumulated snow. If they were fresh out of the oven before, now they would be cold.

Just as Fern reached for the plate and began to reply in gratitude, the littlest child tore away from her mother's shushing hands and dashed into the garage, behind Fern.

Panic ensued. A panic Fern hadn't recently encountered. A sort of *welcome* panic. The two older children dashed into the garage, too, as if pandemonium was permission to cross a line.

The mother apologized briefly before screaming "Briar Beth Engel, get back here *right now*!"

Of course, that was useless, and Fern was unsure how to react other than laugh.

"Um," she began as the woman strode past her and through the maze of boxes to the deepest corner of the garage. "Be careful," Fern called weakly after her. She turned to see the other two children poking through an open box. "Excuse me," Fern intoned, her laughter falling off and her voice turning thick with anxiety. "No snooping, please."

The children seemed to ignore her entirely and turned their attention to the shelf behind them where a collection of glass bells perched in a row. The husky child picked up a bell and shook it. Too hard.

"Put that down," Fern hissed, uncomfortable with scolding another woman's child and losing any patience she thought she had.

At last, the mother and toddler reappeared, the toddler kicking her legs in babyish furor, her little face red and mottled with either melted snow or tears. Maybe both.

"Sorry about that, Fern," the woman said as she wrapped her arms around the little thing, effectively restricting further movement.

Fern let out a small sigh and tried to shake her head in assurance that everything was okay. Everything was okay.

"Dakota, put that back!"

Fern spun to catch the little cookie carrier lift the tarp from a pile of boxes. *Dakota* dropped the flap and yawned in boredom. "Why is there so much crap in here?"

"Dakota, go back home and wash your mouth out with soap. What is wrong with you, child?" the mother scolded before returning her attention to Fern. "So how have you been?"

Fern turned to the woman, incredulous that she was attempting a normal conversation in light of their non-existent relationship. Being neighbors didn't mean much when you lived acres apart and preferred to keep to yourself. She nodded slowly. "Fine. How about you, Maggie?"

Fern would never forget the day the Engels moved in. It was a week before Stedman left. It was one of the final straws.

"Don't you know them?" He'd asked, after he and Travis Engel had chatted down by the mailboxes.

Fern had stood at the window, peering out between a slit in the lace curtains.

When he'd returned inside and asked her, she shook her head.

"They're close to our age. Let's invite them over." It was less of a suggestion and more of a challenge.

Again, she shook her head.

"How do you not know these people? In a small town? Where you both grew up? Don't you want friends, Fern?"

Chapter 7

Fern knew that Maggie wanted to come inside, though more out of curiosity than neighborliness. She wanted to snoop. She wanted to see just how weird Fern was. Just how strangely she lived among all those boxes and all that stuff and all those *things*.

The two older children had both left. They could be heard squabbling only as far as halfway down the drive. The snow muted their argument.

Frost from atop the cookies had long melted, leaving a small puddle on top of the plastic wrap.

"Um, I would invite you in, but I haven't cleaned the house this week. Laundry day, you know," Fern offered, finally.

She kept her eyes trained on the cookies, tilting the plate just enough to clear away the melt.

Chocolate chip. Her mother's favorite.

"Oh, my house is a disaster. Remember, Fern, I have four heathens for children." She smiled at the bundle of joy who was currently pouting in her arms then nuzzled the child with her nose before going on. "And, well, you've probably heard all there is to hear about Travis. He's a useless husband who claims to work around the clock. His empty beer cans prove that's never the case. Ha!" Maggie snorted and jostled the toddler into a new position and then opened her stance toward the door into the house. Expectant.

Fern glanced up from the cookies and then studied the child. Cherubic cheeks and icy eyes squished together under a too-big knitted cap. No one could fault Maggie for her motherliness. Despite the woman's garish makeup and plastic effects, her children were cared for. Fern smiled at the little girl, whose pruney face softened in reply.

"Aw, now would you look at that? She likes you, Ms. Monroe." Again with the jostling.

Fern locked eyes with Maggie and wondered why she was vacillating between formality and familiarity.

Maggie lifted a painted eyebrow, reminding Fern that she invited herself inside.

"It's really a mess. But if you'd like to share the cookies, I'll go get a couple glasses of milk. We can sit in here. I have Adirondack chairs somewhere around here," Fern announced at last, searching the area in earnest. Her tongue passed over her lips as she waited for Maggie and little Briar to take their cue and exit.

They did not.

Instead, Maggie beamed back. "Great idea. Briar can play in the snow right there—" she pointed toward the empty expanse of fresh snow in the drive. "We'll set up here and have a nice little chat."

Maggie pulled her hood off and set the child down, patting her on the bottom as a means to push her off into the snow. Then, Maggie traipsed across the garage toward the back, where stacks of plastic chairs—not the Adirondack ones—loomed in on each other in all their dry rot glory.

Maggie grabbed the top chair and tugged it free from the pile.

Fern frowned but set the cookies down and went inside to fetch a couple glasses of milk. She returned quickly.

"I hope you won't mind my asking, Maggie, but... why are you doing this?" Fern asked, keeping her voice light as she passed two squat glasses of milk her way.

Maggie grabbed a second chair and positioned it just so—adjacent to the first one, creating a neat bistro effect with oil spots as decorative flooring between them. "Why am I bringing cookies and sitting down for a chat in the snow?"

Fern nodded, her face frozen in a sweet—if subtle—southern smile.

The blonde woman sank into a plastic chair. "Honestly?" she asked, facing Briar who was plodding along in a zigzag as the snow began to lessen.

Fern breathed a sigh of relief. She'd hate for little Briar to get too cold and wet. Nothing was worse than being cold and wet at the same time.

She felt Maggie staring at her as she bit into a cookie.

"Oh, yes. I mean, well, I appreciate it, of course. But I'm just surprised. We don't really..." Fern grew tense just then. "Interact." She winced at her awkward accusation and discreetly wiped chocolate chip cookie crumbs from her chin with her sleeve, embarrassed by her show of poor manners.

Maggie sighed. "I'll tell you why I'm here, Fern. If I didn't bake more cookies, I'd have eaten all the cookie dough and been glued to the toilet for the night. And once we had another batch of cookies, I knew I had to get rid of them. No offense, Fern. But there you have it. It was an act of desperation." Maggie smiled coyly as Fern belted out a laugh and reconsidered everything she knew.

She thought back to a few months prior. When Maggie and her friend—Becky Linden, was it?—turned up with a question about someone they thought Fern knew. Maggie seemed scared, really. Even now, the woman was edgy. Maybe she wasn't here to snoop. Maybe she was here for some other reason. *Other* than the threat of a cookie dough tummy ache.

Fern eased into the open seat and watched Briar shuffle through snow. "Well, I just figured you... I figured no one was comfortable coming here. Visiting me." She felt her cheeks grow red from the admission.

"Well, we're not. But I have no self-control when it comes to baked goods *or* unbaked goods, and being stuck inside with three kids will drive a woman to do things she normally wouldn't. So here I am, Ms. Monroe. By the way, you aren't much older than me, and we basically know each other. Should I keep calling you Ms. Monroe?"

Fern chuckled then eyed Maggie. "Technically, it's *Mrs. Gale.*"

***

"I had no idea you were married." Mild shock filled Maggie's face. Briar, taking notice of a delicate shift between the women in the garage, toppled backward and plopped into the snow. A cry floated away from her mouth.

Maggie's previous put-on familiarity dissipated somewhat, though Fern wasn't sure why.

"I suppose I keep to myself, really," Fern answered, her gaze following Briar in her pursuit of pushing up from the snow despite the added layers of puff about her squat body.

A giggle spilled across the garage. Maggie pressed a hand to her mouth. "Sorry, I'm not laughing at you. It's just this girl," she interrupted, pointing to Briar and letting out another self-satisfied laugh.

Fern smiled, unsure if she was still invited to explain herself.

Maggie rose from her chair and strode out to the snowy patch where she righted Briar and patted wet snow from the girl's bottom.

The sky was still gray, but the clouds had seemingly dumped all they needed to. A frigid chill swept up from the street. Fern shivered.

Maggie returned to her seat and eased back in, but Briar ran in behind her, apparently irritated by the lack of snowflakes to catch in her soggy mittens.

"Here, let me take those," Maggie said, reading Fern's mind as she tugged the damp cotton from the little girl's hands.

The child chugged her glass of milk, still unsatisfied. "I'm hun-gy," Briar whined.

Maggie bounced the shivering girl on her leg as though she were an infant and then looked to Fern. "We'd better be going soon. She's got serious 'hanger' issues. Takes after me in that respect." As she said it, Maggie clawed the air with one set of her fake nails, half of a set of air quotes.

Fern frowned. Though she didn't want the company, she found she was anxious to tell someone about Stedman. Anyone. It had not occurred to her that her short-lived marriage never penetrated the gossip circles in Hickory Grove.

Surely Maggie Engel would be at the top of that sort of chain. Wouldn't she want to savor a bit of drama, particularly drama that came from her hermit neighbor?

Here she was, this woman who'd never so much as waved up at Fern's house, claiming she wanted to unload some cookies, unaware that her own neighbor had, indeed, married a man. But she was ready to leave. Maggie might be more of an enigma than Fern.

"Well, if she's hungry, she's welcome to the cookies," Fern tried, holding the plate up from her lap."

Maggie eyed them, likely considering their nutritional value and weighing that against the opportunity for gossip.

Fern began to stand to go inside. She was silly to want to lure this woman and her toddler into the history of her life. Silly to so much as sit and chat.

"Maybe another time," she said, at last. But Briar had popped up from her mother's lap and leapt toward the plate of cookies, squirming her hand beneath the limp plastic wrap and ensnaring two, soft rounds then backing slowly away like a rascally animal.

Maggie burst out laughing at the scene. "She wins. She always does," she said after her laughter tapered off. Then, to Fern's surprise and pleasure, Maggie leaned back into the chair and ran her hands along her thighs.

Fern wasn't sure if this was a joke she, too, could laugh at. A mother who had no control of her child. A child who stole. Then again, everything didn't need to be so serious. Were they in a movie, Fern most certainly would chuckle along with the laugh track. She blinked, and her face softened but she didn't pick up her story where she left off—or rather, before she'd even begun.

But Maggie was a smart woman. And a kind woman, after all. "I can't believe we've lived next door for *years* and never spoken to one another," she said.

Fern lifted an ungroomed eyebrow and nodded. "I'm...reclusive."

"Some people in town think you're dead," Maggie answered, throwing a sidelong glance at Fern as though, in fact, she might be dead.

At that Fern *did* laugh. Hard. And it felt *good*.

"Hickory Grove isn't that small, but it's small enough that no one trusts a stranger, you know. I suppose people here just came to think of you as a stranger," Maggie added pointedly.

Fern accepted that. And she saw an opening. "Well, my husband didn't stick around, anyway. We had a place together in Louisville for almost a year then came back here to buy a home and settle down. We even lived here for a spell. You know, while we were looking for a place. To take care of my mother, too. Then Mom died, and he left soon after."

A quietness filled the garage, wrapping them awkwardly, neither one certain where to take the conversation next. It confirmed for Fern the one thing she was glad to know: that Maggie understood. Maggie, it seemed, understood *everything* in that quiet, awkward moment.

And any explanation for Stedman—for who he was and why he left—perhaps mattered less.

By the time the quiet had gone on long enough that it was no longer awkward, Briar returned from munching happily on the two cookies.

"Can I may please have more?" She pieced together the sentence with intention and hope. Fern smiled down at her then glanced across to Maggie.

"No, you may please can not have more," Maggie tsked. She laughed with Fern. "You can go back and play in the snow a little while longer. Make a snowman for us, Bri," she instructed.

Briar, surprisingly, didn't protest her mother's answer and toddled away into the snow, somehow aware of exactly what she ought to do. Maybe all children were born knowing about things like snowmen. It was just the natural way of childhood.

"Do you have any other family in town?" Maggie asked, finding a natural rhythm for their chat.

Fern shook her head and slipped a cookie, testing a corner then nibbling away in silence.

Maggie nodded. "My parents are gone, too. My aunt raised me and my brother. Marguerite Devereux. I think you two knew each other?"

At that, Fern's face lifted. "Yes. She and my mom were seamstresses together. Remember?" She looked hard at Maggie, willing the woman to recall this long-lost connection.

Maggie's eyes widened. "Yes!" She exclaimed. "That's right! I remember your mom passed along Christmas gifts for us. She was like a silent benefactor of little knickknacks and Christmas crafts. How could I have forgotten?" Maggie's face fell into a hard frown.

Fern shrugged her shoulders and took a sip of milk.

"So how did you meet him?" Maggie went on.

"Who?" Fern asked, eyeing Briar as she toddled from the driveway and into the mounds of snow drift that covered rusted lawn ornaments. "Be careful, there, dear!" she called out to the little girl.

Maggie stood to go redirect Briar as she answered over her shoulder, "Your ex-husband."

Once Maggie and Briar had returned, Briar wriggling violently in Maggie's arms, Fern realized their time was almost up.

She stood to acknowledge the inevitable then opened her mouth to reply to Maggie's question. "Oh, he's not my ex. We're still married."

Chapter 8

Fern felt lame for revealing her secret to Maggie, whose face twisted in confusion before she answered.

"Oh?" the bottle-blonde asked. "But you're not together..."

Fern shook her head in time for Briar to burst out sobbing for no good reason.

Maggie shushed Briar, and Fern could tell she would have liked to stay and hear more.

It was all Fern needed to let them go. Maggie's interest in her life in her life was enough to make her day.

But she read the situation and assured her neighbor they'd get together sometime. Now that the ice was broken.

Dragging Briar through the snow, Maggie waved hopefully and trudged down the long, snow-encrusted drive and an acre up the street—over to the Engel home which suddenly felt farther away than it had before.

Children must do that. Make things seem farther. Harder. Longer. More tiresome.

She was tired just watching poor Maggie wrestle with the little monkey.

Fern sighed, happy in spite of herself.

Now aware of just how much shopping she'd accomplished, she realized she'd have to leave the bags and boxes for another day. She was exhausted and dying to unwind after having *company*.

Fern giggled to herself at the thought—*company*.

Maybe a little Christmas magic was just the thing she needed to shake things up. Maybe pushing herself to open up would help her heal. Four years was enough. Enough time to get over her mother's death *and* her husband's absence. Right?

Sometimes, Fern indulged herself with self-pity over the latter incident. She'd replay the circumstances leading up to Stedman's arrival home from work: in his hands, a limp bouquet; in his eyes, exhaustion.

"Are we going out?" He had asked.

She'd been confused. They never went out. They stayed in. They were homebodies. And Eleanor had only died a couple months before. *"Why would we go out?"* She had replied.

His reaction came as a shock but also a relief.

He dropped the wilted bouquet to the floor and simply left, turning on his heel, opening the door, shutting it behind him. Fern assumed he'd return. Maybe in an hour.

Four hours had passed before she gave up and went to bed where she lay awake for another four hours.

He hadn't returned by the next morning, when it occurred to her that it was their wedding anniversary. Or rather, that the day before had been their wedding anniversary.

One year of marriage.

And he left.

A month went by and still no Stedman. He hadn't even returned for his belongings. Not a pair of underwear or the wrist watch she'd given him after their vows. Nothing.

It was then that Fern quit the museum. She rounded out her extended leave of absence with a formal two-week notice. Her boss said he understood. After all, her mother's death and her husband's abandonment were enough to convince anyone that Fern was a charity case.

Eleanor's inheritance would have tided her over for some time, but the anxiety medication and sleeping pills lost their effectiveness anyway. Fern's depression turned into a taxing sort of boredom.

She had to do something.

Fern couldn't very well show her face in town again, not after losing her husband so quickly (it never occurred to her that no one really knew or cared that she *was* married).

The only option was to work from home. It didn't have to pay much—not at first. It just needed to keep her mind busy. Busy enough to stop with the meds and busy enough to settle back in to some of her old pastimes—watching movies and tinkering around the house as Toffee lazily watched on.

Being adept with search engines, she stumbled across various options.

Only one spoke to her: brokering antique transactions online.

It was a new marriage for her: a marriage of convenience and of passion—her joy in working with things of yore and her need to slip deeply into her mother's world. A world in which she curated those *things* her mother and her father and their mothers and fathers and the ones before had left behind.

Eventually, she hoped to run her own antique shop. That would be the day.

Of course, all this meant Fern could never rid the home of any of its valuables (and *everything* felt valuable).

No, no. She'd have to bring in new old things, and the new old things could be the ones she would one day carefully photograph and upload—the ones for which she would oversee bidding wars. One day.

In the meantime, she helped other people do that.

Now that her company had disappeared into the distant snow, Fern began her evening routine.

Once inside, she slipped out of her heavy coat and long sleeves and ducked into the shower. Moments later, tied into her old robe, Fern made her way through to the kitchen for her "nightcap" before switching on the Christmas lights and then tucking herself into the cushions of the sofa for a marathon of made-for-TV Christmas movies.

Toffee, however, hadn't made her presence known yet. Fern didn't try to micromanage the cat, but it was a rare occasion that Toffee wasn't already snoring on the couch by the time Fern would sit down for a movie.

"Toffee? Here girl," Fern called from the sofa.

The little fluff pranced around the corner and leapt up into Fern's lap. The two fell into a cuddle as green and red and silver and gold flashed across the screen.

For the first time in years, Fern's heart began to fill.

Maybe, Toffee alone wasn't enough. Maybe her movies weren't enough. But if she were ending an otherwise cheery day with Toffee *and* Hallmark *and* a new friend, then, well, that was surely enough.

Chapter 9

Loud voices stirred Fern from a particularly deep sleep. She twisted into the back cushions of the sofa and buried her head, tugging the blanket around her shoulders and willing herself back into a dream.

An all-too familiar ache crawled up the back of her neck. She never did schedule an appointment with the chiropractor after throwing her back out one day late last spring.

The ache would likely turn into a full-blown migraine if she didn't shut off the television, shake two aspirin into her mouth and gulp down a glass of cold water.

Fern pressed her fingers into her temples and then moved them to the base of her neck where she massaged the hollow there for some moments before finally pushing up into a sitting position with her legs tucked under. She squinted at the glare of the screen.

An infomercial blasted out commands at what *must* have been a greater volume than usual. The promoter in his polo shirt standing at a waist-high counter was downright yelling at her.

She had to act fast. Shielding her eyes from the piercing blue backlight, Fern twisted her body and let her feet find purchase on the knotted rug below.

It was still dark outside, and she expected it must be past midnight (the infomercial) and well before dawn. Although, in winter, the sun would not rise in Indiana until nearly eight o'clock.

Still, the clanging of the product promoter coupled with the early signs of a migraine transported her to some bizarre dimension where she had to remember her bearings and navigate them like an explorer.

She'd forgotten about the new dresser she'd just brought in from Hickory Grove Collectibles and walked right into it on her way out of the living room.

"Ouch," Fern grumbled, one hand shielding her eyes from the blue flashing and the other hand groping for a way around the intruding furniture. Finally, she made it out of the great room and into the hallway that would eventually take her to the kitchen.

313 Pine Tree Lane was a big house.

Too big, some people accused, as though there was a morality about just how big a house you could own if you were single and without children. At least Fern had Toffee to help fill the space.

Despite her packrat tendencies, she still tried to keep a general organization scheme. *A room for everything and everything in its room*, she told herself.

Crafting and sewing projects were housed in the red room (so-called because of its fading red wallpaper).

Office supplies and paperwork, including banker boxes and footlockers with important documents, found a home in the office, of course. After all, it was the smallest of the four bedrooms and lacked the expansive windows that really deserve position in a *bed*room. Plus, it had no closet.

Then again, neither did Fern's own bedroom. Instead, she used her great-grandmother's wardrobe. It was a turn-of-thecentury piece hewn, built, and stained by Lena's husband and Fern's great-grandfather. Fern intended to refurbish it soon.

Living in southern Indiana, one needed outfits for all four seasons. And since neither Eleanor nor Fern saw much sense in disposing of Granddad Monroe or Mamaw's best garments, a whole room was dedicated to Monroe Couture, as Fern liked to call it. So, what may have been a child's playroom or a nursery instead became the dressing room. Complete with Mamaw Monroe's oval cheval mirror and a tufted bench.

Fern tried very hard to keep the red room, the office, her bedroom, and the dressing room just as they were meant to be. Yes, she would bring in a piece or two that she'd find in the basement. Perhaps she'd move a piece from another part of the house into one of these rooms if it suited her. Otherwise, they were full of Monroe collectibles only.

Stedman, during the brief time he'd lived in 313 Pine Tree Lane, also had his own office. The same one he'd left without so much as a cursory inspection.

Even after he'd gone, Fern respected his privacy. Mostly, she supposed, she was afraid to go in and explore. Afraid to find something. Know something. Stedman had been an open book during their marriage, however. So, likely, there was nothing to find or know. She knew him well enough.

But as she began to collect more and more, she needed his room. And so, it was something of a storage space. The rug beneath his sturdy oak desk was covered in antique rotary phones, and a couple typewriters. But she was careful to leave a path to and from his desk.

Just in case.

On the first floor, Fern eventually designated the parlor as her business room. That's where she kept her computer and would organize and pile those other people's collectibles for her curating and resale. Currently, she was dealing antique instruments. She'd spent the last few weeks negotiating a contract for a Louis XV upright piano. It inspired her to keep an eye out for instruments that she could one day sell. So far, she'd amassed a banjo, a violin, and a vintage harmonica.

Eleanor's room was the only one that hadn't grown plump with more things. In fact, Fern treated it with more caution than she ever treated the Dotson museum. A museum, eventually, took on more pieces. And perhaps lost some in trades or in inter-museum lending. Eleanor's room was more a crypt, perhaps. All that was missing was the woman's taxidermied, lifeless body sinking beneath the afghan duvet.

Fern headed to the downstairs bath to first grab her pills.

The hall was dark and the glow of the television had puttered out at the bathroom doorway, but she couldn't stand to turn a light on. It might be the one thing to push her growing ache past the point of no return. So instead of fumbling for a switch, she ran her hand along the top of the wainscoting.

As she neared the hall bath, Fern began to register a new sound. Something louder than that of the television set. If she didn't know any better, she'd think it was running water. *Rushing* water even.

Sure enough, as she arrived just outside the bathroom door, her socks grew cold and soggy.

Confused and with her headache growing by the moment, Fern grabbed the aspirin bottle from the medicine cabinet, tossed the pills into her dry mouth and swallowed them as well as she could without water.

She braced herself for catastrophe as she left the bathroom and stood in the hall, on what was most assuredly a wet hardwood floor.

She took two more steps and flipped the hall light switch.

At the end of the hall was the laundry room. There, beyond the washer and dryer sat a basin sink, secured to the exterior wall.

Fern's eyes slowly adjusted to the maddening scene.

Behind and beneath the basin sink, water was spraying from the wall directly into the side of the washing machine. Water had filled the floor, and Toffee sat on what had become something of a beach, on the threshold where the hallway met the room. She was dipping her paw into the frigid water and then licking it off as though she'd stumbled across a fresh mountain spring. Cats, Fern decided in that moment, were nothing if not aloof to disaster.

Fern's head throbbed anew and a sharp pain shot down her back. She tried to make sense of the tragic scene but couldn't.

Careful to avoid Toffee as she sat content and happy, Fern tiptoed around the growing lake to get a better view and to see why water was shooting out from the basin and directly into the washing machine.

Of course.

A burst pipe.

Fern wracked her brain. She'd never had a pipe burst. Ever. Were the pipes never updated? Could it be from the storm?

When Fern was a girl, a pipe had burst at her aunt's house in New Albany. The way it had been explained then was that the pipes froze up then thawed out, expanding and popping the pipes like a British Christmas cracker.

She had come in later than usual that night. She had turned the heat up, too. It might explain such a disaster.

Fern shook her head, carefully. Her eyes began to water as she stormed back through the hall to the sofa to find her phone.

She placed three calls. One to the water service provider. No answer. She left a message on the emergency line. And two to Hickory Grove plumbers. No answer. She left two more messages.

The next step, and it had to happen soon, was to kill the water supply. But, of course, Fern had no clue where the water shut-off valve would be.

Her mother had known. And her father before her. An emergency repairman wouldn't arrive for at least an hour—maybe much longer. Maybe not until the next morning. Especially in a little place like Hickory Grove. Then again, Fern could always go outside in the dark and the snow and start hunting, but the task seemed insurmountable.

She felt her throat begin to close from the stress. Tears bubbled up at the base of her eyelids.

She was alone with no one to help. No one who knew the layout of her home.

But, then, Fern was wrong.

There was *one* person who knew the Monroe family home.

Stedman Gale.

Chapter 10

"Hello?" Stedman grumbled into the line.

Fern's heart stopped for a moment.

His voice was bedraggled and rough. Rougher than she recalled. She glanced at the clock above her television set. A quarter past four.

Blinking away fresh tears, she stood up from the arm of the sofa and paced the hall near the laundry as though her mere presence would prevent the water from pooling further.

"Hi," she said, her voice quaking.

Of course Fern didn't expect him to recognize her voice. Not at this hour. Not anymore. She expected nothing more than for him to hang up on her. But she was desperate.

"Fern? Is that you?" He cleared his throat as her heart dropped down into the bottom of her stomach and boomeranged back up to the top of her chest.

"Yes, hi. I'm so sorry to bother you this early." She glanced at the time again, waiting for a click and a dial tone. Or at least a scoff.

More confused than irritated, it seemed, he replied, "Are you okay?"

Fern composed an image of Stedman in her mind's eye. He'd be in bed. Maybe not even his own. Maybe a hotel room bed for work. Shirtless, as he preferred to sleep in boxers only. His hair would be tousled—assuming the transition to his mid-forties didn't take that from him. His five o'clock shadow would have advanced nearly to the point of short beard by this time of the morning.

She shook the thought. "Yes," she started. Then, her reality cut a sharp angle across her brain. Again, the tears crept up to the edges of her inner eyelids. "No," she breathed through the phone, her composure lost to a new fit of sobs.

Aware he might be afraid of the worst, she choked out a better answer. "There's water everywhere. A pipe burst or something. The house is starting to flood. Oh, Stedman. Please help me."

It was the cry of an estranged wife who never found another man. Or a friend. Or anyone to fill the void. Then again, a vision of Maggie with chubby little Briar helped to ease the sorrow. Fern wasn't *totally* alone. She did have a neighbor. And that neighbor had a husband.

She opened her mouth to beg off the call and correct this whole scenario. She'd walk over to Maggie's place. She'd be humiliated at waking near-strangers at this hour. She'd be even further humiliated to have them see her messy house, but it wasn't *that* bad, really.

"It's in the front yard. Down by the street on the north corner. A green riser, Fern. Look for the green riser then call a plumber. I can't help you."

And just as brusquely as he'd answered, he met her expectations. He hung up.

***

After quelling another fit of sobs, Fern again placed a call to the water service and the two plumbers, this time leaving more frantic pleas for help.

The idea of asking Maggie and Travis for help again passed through her head. The problem was, however, they didn't know where this riser was either. And on a literal acre of snow-buried front yard, Fern would wind up with two new enemies rather than two new friends.

So, Fern suited up in thermal underwear, snow boots, and her winter gloves. She opted out of jacket and pants in order to have better range of motion. Who knew what a green riser was and what it would require of her?

The water seeping along the corners of the hallway now, Fern ducked outside into the predawn morning with her trusty flashlight in hand. It wasn't snowing, but the dark sky felt heavy and low as she tramped through her front yard junk, grabbing the snow shovel en route. She knew she'd seen a green lid somewhere by the street before. She beelined out.

First she dug around the inside of the drive, aimlessly scooping and tossing shovelfuls of snow this way and that before lifting the flashlight in an urgent and pitiful search.

Fern had perhaps never felt so alone in her entire life.

After shoveling clear to the earth on the inside of the garage, she wiped moisture from her face with the back of her glove, doing little to dry the tears and the sweat and the snow.

Then, rubbing the glove across her lower back, she paused. Here she was, in her forties with no friends, standing in her long johns at the foot of her drive as the interior of her house flooded.

Sadly, it became clear the exterior was no better, really. The dull Christmas lights from ages ago didn't add anything. In fact, they detracted. Blown-out bulbs were more obvious than she realized they would be. Yard trinkets and furniture bent this way and that, peeking up through the snow like wooden weeds.

How had she arrived here? Was it fate? Was this the penalty for taking good care of one's mother, befriending her and obeying her? Was this where Fern's good deeds had gotten her?

She tossed the shovel down and melted into the snow. She gave up.

The house would slowly, over time, become a total loss once the water made its way into the great room and the kitchen and the parlor.

"*Oh, no,*" she whispered to herself. "*The parlor.*" All her collectibles sat on the floor in the parlor. Neatly in little sections, organized by type and value.

At least the parlor was on the opposite side of the house from the laundry room. She had a little time to salvage her things.

Another sob crawled up her throat as an all-consuming helplessness took over. Maybe she could move into the Hickory Grove independent living home. Was there an age minimum? They might appreciate a relative youngster bringing down the average, right?

Now freezing and wet, she realized she couldn't simply sit out in the snow on her knees. It wouldn't be the independent living home they'd put her in. It'd be a whole other kind of facility.

Exhausted and depressed, it occurred to her that her headache had vanished. That was enough to inspire Fern to start digging on the other side of the drive. She had to be close to the water shut-off. It's not like utility companies hid these things.

It was just the snow she had to move. And dawn was on her side. It would only grow lighter. Eventually. If the plumber or water company didn't show up before then.

Fern grabbed the shovel and slogged through the snow closer to the street. Her thermal underwear clung to her butt and created a highly uncomfortable, soggy diaper effect.

She'd better hurry.

After twisting in a quick stretch, she got back to it, throwing all her might into swooping up high piles of snow and displacing them.

Only moments into excavating, she felt headlights splash across her back and careen around her damp form, finally spraying onto her house.

Finally. Someone to help. She'd pay them whatever they charged. Anything to stop the flood and *be with her* during this trauma.

She turned and waved blindly into the bright glare then scooped another shovelful, unwilling to stop now. Every moment counted. One minute could be the difference between tearing up all the hardwood floor and only tearing up a hallway of it.

The service person left his vehicle running with its lights directed on her, which added a new gravitas to the project.

Her back was turned to the approaching man and she could hardly hear him over the blood pounding in her ears and the hum of his engine.

"Here, let me!" he shouted and tore the shovel from her. At last, she looked up at him to thank him and explain what happened.

But he didn't look at her, instead he took the shovel and stomped through the snow past her, closer to the far corner of where her property line abutted the adjacent street.

He knew exactly where to go, and it wasn't because he was a local plumber or the night shift guy for Hickory Grove Water.

He was her husband.

Chapter 11

Fern followed in disbelief, watching in awe as he kicked through snow until he found the green riser.

He hadn't dressed for the circumstances, and though he did wear snow boots, his sweats were soaked up to the knees. A UofL hoodie hardly concealed his build and it was clear that a few years did little to affect his fitness.

Thanks to the bright headlights, Fern took note that his hair—though tousled—was still thick and as dark brown as ever.

While Stedman shoveled, a realization took hold of her. She was out there in thin long johns. And though Stedman appeared evergreen, she most certainly was not. Her hair would be matted to the side of her head, no doubt. No makeup. She had enough crows' lines for the both of them.

Her southern manners kicked in, and Fern stomped up to his position next to the riser as he dropped on his knees and twirled around a tool made of rebar.

"Let me help," she offered as she came up behind him. He shook his head, but she bent next to him. As she did, Stedman finally lifted his eyes to hers.

The man she'd decided to hate for so long was now within inches of her face. The man who had left her. The man who never looked back. Now, here he was. At once a foreigner, and enemy, and yet a friend.

His expression unreadable, he offered a tight-lipped smile. A smile that would like to reach his eyes but fought it. She could see in him a question. A question she didn't have the answer for.

Her gaze dropped from his clear blue irises down to his mouth. She was right. Stubble shadowed his jaw and the lower half of his face, framing his lips in a rugged, appealing effect.

The moment came as fast as it went and he dropped the tool into the riser.

Anxious to do something—anything—to help, she grabbed for the green lid which he'd tossed a few feet off. As she did, her foot caught on a hidden rock and flew, face first, into the snow.

"Oh, Fern," came Stedman's voice behind her. "Are you okay?"

As if she needed any more saving that night, she waved him off from inside of a veritable snowbank. A brief second passed, and she squirmed around in time to watch Stedman toss his tool and take a wide step to her.

For the second time now, they locked eyes. He wiped the back of his hand across his forehead, his mouth set in a frown. Blood pulsed through her veins as he neared, but she pushed the sensation away and pulled herself up into a sitting position.

Still, he bent forward and cupped his hands around the very top of her ribcage and began to pull her up.

Caught off-guard by this, Fern's first instinct was to bat him away. "I'm fine. I'm fine," she hissed, uncomfortable and titillated and confused. But as she wriggled to get herself up and away from his grip, her heel—which was now wedged beneath her butt—caught again on some unseen natural feature and she tripped forward and into his knees much like a lineman takes out a running back.

Stedman lost his balance and, with his boots securely fastened to the earth by a foot of snow, fell backwards in a quiet thud.

Fern, who was now on all fours in front of him, lunged toward him to apologize. But as she neared, laughter rose from her chest and spilled over him. A deep laugh. A long-suppressed laugh. The kind of laugh that a woman has when her husband looks ridiculous, even if it's her own fault that he came to look ridiculous. Especially when it's her fault.

Stedman, however, was not *really* her husband anymore. And Stedman was not laughing. Not at first. But, his sour expression was difficult to maintain, apparently, and his mouth curled up in a smile at her as her laughter quieted.

"I'm sorry, Stedman," she whispered, her grin fading a little.

His expression dropped again, too. "It's fine," he muttered, pushing himself up and offering her a hand. This time she accepted. "I got it shut off. You're good to go. If you haven't yet, call a plumber, like I said." He brushed snow from his butt and then clapped his gloved hands together as if to leave.

But, he didn't.

An awkward pause rested between them. He was soaked and (assuming he still lived in Louisville) had a thirty-minute drive ahead of him. Fern would be cruel not to invite him in. She owed him as much after his selflessness.

"Why don't you come in and dry off?" The suggestion took her by surprise. It must have taken him by surprise, too.

Stedman frowned more deeply then shook his head with some degree of vigor. "No, no. I won't impose. I only came because I know Hickory Grove. I knew someone wouldn't get out here until nine in the morning. I didn't want the house to flood. That's all." His eyes darted from her and he leaned over and wiped at the bottom of his sweats as though he could wipe the wetness away.

Fern smiled. "It might not be safe for you to drive back. The roads must be slick. It's still dark. Come in, Stedman. My mother would never forgive me if I didn't offer you fresh clothes and a coffee." She regretted it as soon as she said it.

For Fern to mention her dead mother was akin to off-handedly mentioning the mistress who ignited the downfall of a marriage. Maybe even worse.

A new tension took hold of them, cementing him in place and sending a chill up Fern's spine. The warmth she'd previously felt dissipated. In its place was a new cold.

"I'm sorry. What I meant was, I would like to thank you for this." She waved vaguely around them at the displaced snow.

He seemed to consider his state more than her offer as he pulled at his soaked pant legs and then stretched the wet fabric away from his rear end. After glancing at his truck and back up at the house, he asked, "Do you think you have a pair of pants I could, um, I could... have?"

The implication was clear. He never wanted to return to this place. Borrowing would bring with it an obligation. He would take. Not borrow.

Fern's face fell a little, but she understood. Maybe even felt the same. Their history was nil. She'd give him a change of clothes and say farewell. Never to call him again.

She answered, her voice sad, "Yes, I think I might still have something of yours."

Chapter 12

Once they were inside, Fern invited him to sit in the kitchen. En route, Stedman gawked at the water.

The burst pipe had filled the laundry room with an inch or more and then trickled into the hallway, stopping at each room in its path to check for egress. The hall had become a tributary and the hall bathroom was a lake. Fortunately, the damage stopped there, but that would make for two rooms' worth of damage and potential mold.

Toffee glared at Fern from her refuge on the bay window sill, but when she saw Stedman, she lifted her tail coyly, pounced on to the table then curled her way to his legs, taunting him into an ear scratch. Stedman obliged. Fern looked away. She'd adopted Toffee *after* Stedman left.

The darn cat had no ability to discern a stranger. No sense of character judgment.

"It reminds me of *Titanic*," Fern muttered as she noticed a little rivulet of water had made its way into the kitchen, after all, before puttering out along the baseboards by the back door.

Stedman shook his head, weary. "At least it didn't start upstairs."

"True," she answered.

"Had to be the pipe from the basin. It's practically exposed on the exterior wall. I wonder why it thawed in the middle of the night, though. That makes no sense." He scratched his head. Fern caught him eyeing the coffee pot.

"Maybe that's because I got in a little later than usual and turned the heat up?" she replied.

It was a stretch. She wasn't in *that* late, but if she suggested she was *out and about*, she might seem—more interesting to him. Again she silently chided herself for caring one iota about what Stedman Gale thought of her now.

"Well, until the plumber gets back to you, I'd throw down towels and blankets as fast as possible. Prevent it from seeping. Maybe you can save some of the floor, though I doubt it."

She left him with useless ol' Toffee and sped to the first floor linen closet, pulling two stacks of towels and thrusting them at Stedman, who'd followed.

They worked quickly and—having used almost every towel, sheet, and blanket from the closet—got most of the water sopped up. This was the *only* time Fern was grateful for having a small laundry room.

"Can I get those pants?" Stedman asked, as they finished up. "Maybe a shirt, too?" He visibly shivered.

Fern nodded. "Of course. Here, you might as while dry off, first." She passed him the only towel that remained from their clean-up effort.

After a strange little dance in which Stedman lamely pretended he wasn't quite sure he remembered where to head, Fern awkwardly ushered him into the upstairs bath.

She murmured she'd return with an outfit before starting toward his office where boxes of his belongings sat, waiting patiently for this very moment.

Stedman thanked her and stepped inside the bathroom with the towel but then stopped short, chuckling when Fern turned her back.

"I guess some things never change," he said.

Confused, Fern spun around to see her red bra hanging like an ornament from his finger. Her face bloomed into the exact same color as the lingerie, she snatched it out of his hand, and all but sprinted down the hall.

He laughed as she darted off, but she was mortified. In their one year of marriage, he'd never seen her in anything like *that*. What would he think now?

Thank *goodness* it wasn't her nude comfort bra which looked more like a geriatric contraption than women's undergarments.

She quickly found a pair of jeans and returned to the bathroom, where Stedman leaned into the doorframe, now holding a towel in place at his hip. His sweatshirt and pants were folded carefully on the edge of the pedestal sink. His shirt must have been tucked in there, somewhere, too.

Fern swallowed hard and forced herself to focus on his face.

"I'll get out of your hair, Fern. Don't worry about me," he replied as he took the jeans.

The bra still in her hand, she forced herself to smile back at him. "Take your time. And, uh, sorry about this." She waved the bra awkwardly and tried to explain herself. "It's for special occasions." It came out all wrong and Stedman laughed again.

Fern flushed for the umpteenth time that morning and she covered her face with her hands—and the bra—before speeding off like a mall-walker on a Sunday morning.

On her way downstairs, she dashed into her room where she stowed the illicit item and then changed into a pair of black leggings and a white, long-sleeved top. Ridiculously, she considered throwing on makeup but thought better of it, instead twisting her long hair into a messy bun on top of her head.

A dab of perfume later, she was downstairs ahead of Stedman, brewing coffee. Fern asked herself why she was going to any measure to spruce herself up for this man.

Stedman had left her when she was in the depths of her depression, reeling from her mother's death, after all.

"Hey."

She turned from the counter and leaned back into it, the marble cutting into her lower spine. "Hi," she answered.

He stood there, in a flannel and jeans she'd bought for him before her mom got sick. His wet clothes lay neatly across his hands.

"Oh, just a minute. I've got a bag." She dug beneath the sneak for a paper grocery sack and passed it his way. "Coffee?" she offered, gesturing to the percolator.

He scratched his head. "I really ought to be going, Fern. I—" he paused, his eyes catching something behind her.

Fern turned to see Toffee, leaping down from the window once again and sauntering over to him. It was embarrassing, really.

"She's a pretty girl," Stedman murmured and bent over to scratch her ears again.

"Stedman," Fern interrupted the intimate moment between her best friend and worst enemy. "At least take some to go. I'd hate for you to drive back to Louisville groggy. It's not safe." She wasn't lying. Though she hated him, she also cared about him and wouldn't want him to get in an accident.

He gave Toffee a final pat on top of the head, stood, and shoved his hands into his pockets. "All right. I'll take one to go."

Fern smiled and turned toward the pot. It hadn't filled yet. She turned back. "Um, it'll be just a moment. Sorry." Her eyes darted around the room for something to occupy them.

"Okay," he answered, his voice harder.

Maybe reality was finally setting in. His estranged wife had called in the middle of the night. He made the surprising choice to drive nearly half an hour to help her. And here they were, having discussed nothing more serious than the fact that she was still leaving her bras on doorknobs.

She licked her lips and stared at him until his eyes met hers. "Thank you, Stedman."

He met her gaze and rubbed a hand over the lower half of his face. "You're welcome."

Toffee mewed from somewhere else in the house, and Fern wished she had music playing or the television blaring. The silence wrapped them together, and she felt like screaming.

"You know, Fern, maybe you should put a fire on in the great room. It'll help dry things out in there."

A smile pricked at her lips, and she nodded her head. "Good idea."

"Do you have any firewood inside?" he continued, to her great surprise.

Fern wiped an errant tear from her cheek and turned back to him. "It's on the back deck. I can get it. Don't worry about me. I'll get you a mug for the road and then get it going." It was a fib. Fern was terrible at starting fires, for some reason.

"I can help you."

Taken aback, all she could do was nod and open the back door for him.

Soon enough, Stedman was stuffing balled-up newspaper beneath a neat stack of oak logs as Fern held a travel mug of coffee nearby. Finally, the kindling took and flames ran up to the height of the pile.

Fern desperately wanted to transport herself back four years. Will herself to recover more gracefully from her mother's death. Will herself to pull it together in time to enjoy an evening like this with her husband. An early morning fire. Coffee on the sofa. *Miracle on 34th Street* muted in the background as they talked about life.

"Thanks." Stedman's voice cut through her reverie and he took the mug from her.

Fern nodded. "Oh. Stedman, *thank you*. I don't know what I would have done."

In tandem, they both glanced at the clock above the television.

"I knew it would be awhile, but I can't believe the plumber or emergency water company hasn't returned your call by *now*," he said. Fern wondered why he hadn't left yet.

She strode to the little table next to the sofa and looked at her landline for signs of a missed call or message. None. "I can't either. But, you know how it is here. Someone will be by in the morning. I'm certain of it," she assured him.

He nodded evenly and took a sip of his coffee.

"Do you want to sit?" Fern offered, waving to the sofa, hope arresting her chest. The evidence of her sleeping spot was revealed, but she didn't quite mind. A yawn escaped from her mouth. Stedman caught it and yawned, too.

They both laughed quietly. "No, I really need to get back."

"Are you traveling for work still?" All of a sudden, an urgent need to catch up with him took hold of her. She wanted to grab his arms and asked him everything. What had he been doing for nearly four years? Who had he been doing it with? Had he moved on? Was he as angry with her as she was with him? Were either of them angry anymore?

"Not as much. I'm not taking on new clients. Trying to keep things more local. You know, settle down a bit."

Her stomach lurched. He never wanted to settle down when they were together. She nodded.

"Well, good luck, Fern," Stedman answered, turning toward the door.

She followed him, and Toffee suddenly appeared and stalked circle eights around his legs, nearly tripping him through the door. In other circumstances, it would have been funny. Laugh-out-loud funny. But under these circumstances—a tension thick enough to support both their weight during a reunion that made little sense to either—Toffee's shenanigans felt like a stunt.

Fern's cheeks reddened and she made an awkward attempt to shoo Toffee away. Her effort was unsuccessful, but finally the naughty cat mewed in compromise and leapt up onto the table in the foyer.

Stedman scratched her ear one final time.

Was it final? Fern thought.

She lifted her gaze to meet Stedman's. He was staring at her, waiting.

Should she press him to stay? Should she offer the sofa so he could catch a couple hours of shut-eye before the drive back? Should she whip up some buttermilk pancakes and set out the good china?

"Goodbye, Fern," he said at last and pulled the door open for himself.

But still, he hesitated.

"Stedman, wait."

She could have thanked him and bid him farewell. He might have left and never looked back. She might have gotten to say goodbye this time. That would have been enough. She could really move on.

Her mother's Christmas lights glowed on the front porch, framing his height. The scene was at once familiar and unfamiliar.

The furnace shut off, and the fire in the great room popped as a log cracked and fell through the grate.

Then, inexplicably, the southern belle who lived deep in her heart came out. As if she were the desperate heroine in a Tennessee Williams play, she rested a hand on his thick forearm and said in a syrupy voice that she hadn't used in years, "Stedman, why don't we meet for lunch one day? I'd like to repay your kindness."

Chapter 13

He'd said no.

At first.

And she accepted it.

At first.

After all, what *were* they doing? A four-year gap between his abandonment and now? Four years to leave her to her own devices under the cloud of a deep depression? What man—what *person*—could ever right such a wrong?

But, Fern had realized in the split second when she had his full attention before he left her home and dashed away into the blustery early winter night, Stedman had already begun to right such a wrong. Simply by driving in the predawn hours to help her.

It was enough.

Now, days later, she sat on a bar stool in the riverboat.

It was exactly halfway between Hickory Grove and Louisville. Fern had told Stedman she had business in Louisville and was happy to meet him there. But various conflicts popped up, preventing them from committing to a chaste coffee or a platonic lunch.

Between his work schedule and her white lie, it turned out that six o'clock was the best time for both. And they knew quite well that Fern had no business being in Louisville after five.

So the riverboat it was. Dinner. Drinks if things went well.

In truth, Fern *did* have business in Louisville. She needed to Christmas shop for the Ladies Auxiliary. Black Friday had netted her little in that respect. She still had a couple things to pick up from bigger shops than Hickory Grove had to offer. And anyway, she'd been craving a peppermint hot chocolate from The Louisville Tea House. That wasn't her only business, either.

She needed, as well, to shop for herself.

The day after the pipe fiasco, Hickory Grove water showed up. The serviceman moonlit as a private plumber, and he was gracious enough to fix up the pipe before her work day began—fitting a new one in place of the cracked. Still, she'd have to make an insurance claim and get adjusters and contractors out to assess the damage and repair it.

New flooring. Mold mitigation. All that. Two days earlier, such a to-do list might have crippled Fern. But not now. Now, she was nearly delighted by the opportunity for a fresh start. Even if the fresh start began with something as mundane as her laundry room.

The serviceman had eyed Fern's cluttered home. Embarrassed, she explained she was in the middle of a change. That was all there was to be said. But she'd made a mental note to start a full-blown clean-up effort before the insurance adjuster was due in the coming days.

Fern reached around for her clutch—a vintage black leather piece—and withdrew her lipstick, reapplying in the reflection of the brass compact that she'd found inside its silk pocket.

The weather outside was chilly once again, but new snow hadn't fallen since the morning of their reunion. Barry Manilow's "Have Yourself a Merry Little Christmas" vibrated the dimly lit space, made dimmer by heavy pine boughs and wreaths.

Fern had been surprised to learn that the riverboat even had a coat check. She double-checked her clutch for the ticket as she continued to wait.

"Anything else ma'am?" The barkeep asked, indicating her half-full glass of water.

Fern studied it for a moment then looked back to him. "Why, yes. Have you got any mulled wine?" Eggnog sounded good, too. But that wouldn't do. Not now. Maybe later.

He nodded curtly and returned with a lowball glass filled to the brim with a pretty, burgundy-colored liquid. A fresh orange slice curled inside the glass, and a stick of cinnamon rested along the inner rim. Fern took a careful sip and replaced the glass on a thick cardboard coaster touting the name of the barge: The Mark Twain.

Fern reminded herself that she was on the very border of Kentucky and Indiana. She'd technically grown up in the south. Hickory Grove natives spoke with a thick twang and worked the land for a living.

But the Monroe family weren't farmers or ranchers, and that always made Fern feel somewhat different than those around her. Of course, there were many things that made Fern different. Over-educated parents. Oddballs who opted to homeschool their only daughter. Fern finally broke free and attended Hickory Grove High School, where she was in awe of the social butterflies who fluttered around her—Friday night tailgate. Sunday afternoon fish frys. It was a culture she lived in but never participated in.

In many ways, Fern resented her upbringing and felt it hadn't prepared her for lifelong happiness. But she didn't resent her parents for doing what they thought was best. Especially her mother, who—for a very long time—was Fern's best friend.

"Hi." Stedman's voice broke her reflections, but it was his touch on her elbow that caused her to nearly knock over her drink.

She swiveled to face him.

"Sorry I'm late," he went on. She felt his eyes on her. Fern had taken the time to blow out and tease her hair, add light make-up, and select a none-too-tacky red sweater dress that hid her flaws and complemented her curves. The nude hose were perhaps a touch too far, but she *had* read somewhere that Princess Kate had brought nylons back into style.

"No, you aren't late. I came early," she answered.

Stedman gestured toward the dining room. "The hostess set us a table. Are you ready?"

Fern noticed his stilted speech. An unease and formality, as if this were a business transaction.

Still, she accepted the suggestion and followed him with her wine to a dark corner booth that looked out over the water. The song had changed to a slower piece. "Silent Night" took the place of jaunty Barry Manilow.

They sat facing each other. The hostess propped menus in their hands and took Stedman's drink order. Now the menus stood stiffly in each other's line of sight, the sleeved cardstock poised as a sort of double barricade.

Stedman broke the silence. "I haven't eaten here in ages."

Fern rested the menu on the table in front of her and took a sip of her wine. "Neither have I," she replied airily.

Fern and Eleanor used to have dinner on the Mark Twain every so often. It wasn't their favorite place. But it was a place that surely reminded Fern of her mother. She looked around, taking in the dark room. Her eyes landed back on her husband.

She eyed the parts of him she could see on either side of the menu. A stiff, blue button-up, cuffed at the elbows. A watch clipped neatly around his left wrist. Not the watch he'd left behind years ago.

His fingernails were cut short and square and neat. He'd spent the day at the office, no doubt. Her eyes slipped to the outside corner of his side of the table where his knee bobbed compulsively.

"Long day?" she asked, situating her glass onto the fresh coaster. Fern shifted atop the bouncy booth seat and moved her menu to the side.

Stedman flicked a glance up to her over the top of his menu and smiled tightly. "Yeah."

The hostess appeared. "Care for any appetizers this evenin'?" Her southern dialect cut through the well-mannered script. Fern looked to Stedman. Stedman lifted his hand to Fern.

"Fern?" he asked, his voice softer now.

She glanced through the menu, searching for her favorite—calamari.

Stedman cleared his throat before she had a chance to spot it in the appetizers list. "We'll take an order of calamari, please." An impish grin formed on his mouth and Fern felt a rush of wooziness. She looked at her wine glass to confirm she hadn't downed it without remembering.

She hadn't.

The waitress left and returned moments later with a stout glass of bourbon. Fern smiled, but the smile slipped away as she wondered if people ever really changed.

Stedman took a slow sip and, after, shook his head. At last, he met her eyes and seemed to return to himself. No mischief. No edge. Just Stedman.

"I did have a long day, actually. Sorry if I'm being a little antsy," he admitted.

It caught Fern off guard. "That's fine," she replied, burying her face in her wine glass and pretending to study the menu.

Fern realized they were dancing now. One coy, the other moody; ball-step-change, now it was her turn to play the anxious one. A more natural role than the flirty one.

Were they flirting?

Of course, manners demanded she offer him condolences for his bad day and accept his apology. After all, she was the one who dragged him here as a thank you for the pipe incident.

"Oh, that's all right. I'm sorry to hear about your day. Are you still working for The Peterson Company?" *Now* she was prying.

He nodded. "Sure am. I, uh, I got a promotion. Now I manage and have just a core set of clients, which keeps me busy but tied down. Less travel, more stress."

She smiled. "Tied down? That's not quite *you*," Fern replied.

"It wasn't five years ago. Or even three."

The waitress returned with a pretty plate of calamari. "Are y'all ready to order?" She asked, dropping her fancy-restaurant act all together now.

Again Stedman lifted his hand to Fern. She nodded solemnly. "Yes, I'll have the Greek salad, light on dressing," Fern said, reading weakly from the menu.

Stedman scoffed aloud. "You don't even like salad," he teased. "Are you sure you don't want prime rib? Cooked medium? Hold the horse radish?" His eyes narrowed on her then lifted to the waitress like they shared an inside joke.

Fern's pulse quickened and her chest tightened. Did he really remember little things like that? Did they know each other better than she realized? She shook her head, defiant at first. "That's a little heavy. I mean, he's right..." she went on, "but I'll stick to a salad for tonight." Comfortable Fern *would* have ordered and dug into a hearty helping of prime rib. Uncomfortable Fern would probably play with her food more than eat it.

But a plate of calamari later proved otherwise.

She was on glass number two of mulled wine and they had rehashed every sweet memory that came to them.

"Remember when we were living in that apartment in Louisville," Stedman laughed as he said it. "And you said we ought to get two twin beds instead of one queen?"

Fern glowed, her eyes lit up and she played along at the joke. "Yes, I remember saying it would be like *I Love Lucy*, but you thought I didn't want to touch you until our wedding night."

"You didn't!" he roared.

Fern rolled her eyes. "We touched plenty. We touched so much that separate beds would have done us good. After all, I was a lady! Still am, in fact!"

Stedman cackled at that and returned with his own. "We didn't have to live together before the wedding, you know. You were the one who thought I needed some style. Something girly. You put flowers on the back of the darn toilet, Fern!"

They fell into the table toward each other, laughing till they cried.

"You're the one who made me move in with you, and you know it. I would have been happy as a clam to stay put," she all but hollered back, splashing a bit of her wine onto the table and smiling.

Stedman scooted around the booth and wiped it with his napkin. "Well it was either we get our own place or live with your mom until the wedding."

The laughter died off. The joke was over.

As if on some sort of tragic cue, the waitress delivered their dinner. Fern pushed leaves around with her fork. Stedman dutifully cut into his steak, but before he took his first bite, he mumbled, "I'm sorry about your mom, Fern. I don't know why I brought it up."

Fern shook her head and looked up at him, her momentary sobriety giving way to compassion. "It was a joke. It's okay. And, anyways, I agree."

He cocked his head, took a bite then a swing of his bourbon.

Fern grinned down at her plate as she unfolded a jab of her own. "And anyway, Stedman, I never would have bunked up with *your* family. Is Tobias still living at home or did he find someone with an overbearing mom, too?" Her mouth curled into a wicked grin and she raised an eyebrow knowingly.

Stedman put his fork down, wiped his mouth and studied her with mock seriousness. "Maybe you have lightened up, huh?"

She shrugged, and they tried to resume the playful banter from moments before.

As they finished their meals, the waitress returned once again. "Dessert, y'all?" she asked.

Fern began to shake her head, but Stedman asked if she was certain.

"Yes," she answered. And then, "You know, I think I have eggnog and pie back at the house?" It came out like a question.

Wiggling her eyebrow, the waitress replied, "I s'pose any good date never ends with restaurant dessert." She winked at Fern and left to print their bill.

Heat rushed to Fern's cheeks and she peeked over at Stedman, waiting for his reaction. He held up two hands. "I know you weren't inviting me, Fern."

"I don't know why I even said it except to get out of ordering more calories, really. But you're welcome to come up, of course." Hope hung off her words and her lips parted involuntarily.

Stedman wiped his face with his cloth napkin and folded it neatly before pressing it onto the table.

"Fern, this has been good. Nice. Real nice. I've enjoyed talking. Maybe we, ah, have something here."

Her heart leapt and she was willing to say she forgave him and they could move on and it would be fine. Better than fine. Better than ever. She'd clean her house. She'd get rid of stuff. He wasn't traveling. It was their second chance. Christmas gift ideas whirred through her head.

The waitress interrupted his speech, and he took the bill on his far side, preventing her from peeking. A true gentleman. He always was. Until the very end. With the flowers. On their anniversary. The day she'd forgotten. Maybe she'd better apologize for that now. She opened her mouth while he slid his credit card into the plastic pocket.

But he shook his head. "Fern, no. Listen. This is...this is going well. But, I want to be open with you. When you called me about the water leak, well, I had actually been thinking of reaching out to you."

Fern smiled and batted her eyelashes like a teenager.

But Stedman's face fell a little and he swallowed hard before continuing what seemed like a big speech. "Fern, initially, I agreed to meet with you again for a different reason."

She waved her hand, ready to clear the air and sweep him back home for eggnog, pie, and *White Christmas*, but he put his hand over hers. Beating her to the punch.

"Before all this..." he gestured between them. "Fern, I was ready for a divorce."

Chapter 14

"A *divorce*?" she asked, the wine left her head and settled in the bottom of her stomach. Nausea took effect. "A *divorce*?"

Stedman nodded solemnly. "I know. Here we are laughing and happy right now. But, Fern. Four years is a long time of nothing."

She considered his point and found that, in fact, she didn't disagree.

Four years of nothing.

But now, they were having one night of everything.

Still, Fern's pride was such that she refused to be dumped twice, no matter how many times Stedman repeated "*But tonight has been amazing.*"

So, bizarrely, they left it at that. No dessert. No eggnog or pie. Simply a sad goodbye. Even their waitress seemed bewildered as Fern and Stedman stiffly bid each other farewell at the hostess stand.

Fern got in her car and wondered if she could expect to be served divorce paperwork or if *tonight really was amazing*.

She sat there, in her car, for at least thirty minutes, alternating between sipping water from her water bottle and keeping an eye out so as to avoid Stedman finding her there, sitting and clearing her head in the dark. Once she felt well enough, she pulled out of the parking lot and crept carefully up the riverside road and back home.

***

The next morning, Fern woke up more sluggish than usual. The nag of a headache had returned. Toffee kneaded her scalp, which was always irritating. But instead of pushing the cat away, she buried her head deeper into her pillow.

Maybe she had a headache because she actually dragged herself to bed last night rather than sleeping on the sofa as was becoming the usual.

Maybe she had a headache because of the wine.

Or the late night.

Maybe she had a headache because that was the status quo for Fern Gale. Her heart would start to ache with unhappiness and then it would travel to the back of her neck, wrapping the top of her spine in its path to imbed at the base of her skull. Eventually, the ache would reach her temples or the center of her forehead and she'd have to pop aspirin and chug water.

Not today.

Today she refused. If Stedman Gale had been ready to move on, then so was Fern.

She didn't know how, exactly. But she would figure it out.

If her blurry memory served, the adjuster would arrive at eight on the nose. The realization hit Fern like a wrecking ball and she pulled out from Toffee's paws and slung the covers away.

After sliding into a red hoodie and leggings with screen-printed mistletoe, she veered toward the bathroom to throw her hair up into a messy bun.

The previous night's makeup had mottled in the hollows beneath her eyes, so she took a washrag, dampened it with warm water, and rubbed away the evidence of her heartbreak.

Heartbreak? Could Fern even call it that? What did she expect—that she'd go to dinner with the man who'd abandoned her mere months after her mother's death, and then they'd live happily ever after?

No.

Stedman had *his* chance and Fern had *her* chance. They didn't make it work. Simple as that.

Then again, love might expire, but marriage licenses did not.

The doorbell rang.

Fern traipsed downstairs, nearly tripping over Toffee on her way to answer the door.

"Good morning," she sighed at a solid-looking older man who grimaced behind wire-rimmed glasses.

He nodded. "'Mornin'. Chuck Walton with South State Insurance." His southern accent was heavy and he walked like his back hurt. But a neat button down tucked into khakis and topped off with the glasses gave him all the professional aura he needed.

"Come on in," Fern answered, allowing herself to relax. "The damage is back here," she said. "Coffee? I haven't had mine yet and I full-well intend to make a potful."

"Naw, thank you. Just here to do my job and report back if's awright with ya."

Fern smiled and explained the disaster zone to him before heading into the kitchen to set water to boil and toast bread.

Bored and tired, she slumped into a kitchen chair and pulled a magazine from the leaning stack at the far end of the table.

Toffee, who had just finished her breakfast, purred contentedly on the windowsill. A puff of her fur floated over to the table, landing lightly on the cover of the magazine, concealing a beautiful entryway-scape for the December issue. Fern recoiled at the cat hair, plucked it up and carried it to the trash, washing her hands after.

She might not be good at picking things up and putting them away, but Fern was most assuredly a clean person.

So then, why couldn't she just get rid of her crap?

Returning to the table, she opened the magazine and stared at the stunning arrangements. A dining room table set for eight with silverware and china plates. Sprigs of blue spruce peppered a gold runner on top of which were poised pine tree-molded candles in burnished silver holders, a bowlful of oranges and one of pinecones. Red mugs set dutifully at the upper right corner of each place setting.

It was the perfect example of what Fern wanted for her life. She wanted *stuff* and she wanted that *stuff* to magically arrange itself into a tableau fit for a queen. Her mother had always been able to do it. She was a master of holiday decor.

Fern *could be* a master of decor, too. If she made a point to.

But boxes of antiques lined empty bedrooms. Clutter filled any horizontal surface. And none of it worked together to present a scene out of a magazine.

"Ma'am?" A voice called from the hall.

She swept toast crumbs from the table onto the plate and strode out, leaving Toffee to her own devices. "Yes?" Fern replied as she joined the adjuster at the edge of disaster.

Clipboard in hand, he pushed his eyeglasses up his nose. None of him made sense. It was as if a South State Insurance agent asked his grandfather to fill in for the day. And his grandfather happened to be a farmer. But Chuck was neat and tidy and seemed to know what he was talking about.

After he gave a brief explanation of the looming process, Fern thanked him for coming and began to walk him to the front door.

The hallway narrowed as they neared the parlor. Chuck was ahead, his crooked frame slow-going. Fern watched as he glanced into the parlor, and then came to an abrupt stop.

Toffee mewed behind her, as if to push them forward.

"Everything okay?" Fern asked gently.

He twisted his body to face the open parlor door, his rough hand gesturing inside. "I don't mean to pry, but that there banjo looks jus' like my dad's own back from, aw—well, le's see—had to be 'round 1920. Maybe so far as 1940 when he was playin' the most."

Fern smiled. Someone who valued antiques but wasn't quite a collector.

"My father played, too. Not that one. I keep his upstairs. I've purchased a few over the years." She began to explain why but then realized she had no good reason. If there was a reason, it was the same one to explain why she bought anything. A pipe dream.

"Do y'all sell 'em?"

Fern frowned. "Pardon?"

"Do ya sell banjos or somethin'?"

"Do I sell them? Well, no, but—" *I would*, is what she wanted to say.

"How much ya askin'?" he pressed, turning to face her more fully as he pushed the eyeglasses back up his nose.

Fern fell back, landing on Toffee's tail in the process. The cat screeched and darted away. Fern called a listless apology out but it was too late.

"It wasn't for sale," she began as she began to nod involuntarily.

Chuck opened his mouth to reply and held up a hand, but she went on. "Well, actually. What would you pay?"

A sweet, old man smile pulled his lips back against his face and he reached for his wallet. "I collect banjos. So, I'll give ya all I got. Which is..." He counted surprisingly crisp bills from his wallet, and Fern felt her neck grow hot at such a bootlegged exchange.

Five minutes later, Fern and Toffee reunited at the kitchen table. Fern with a fresh mug of coffee, Toffee curled in her lap. One hundred dollars rested next to her magazine. He'd offered three hundred—which made Fern question just how much an insurance adjuster's salary really was.

She refused the offer and accepted one hundred. It felt fair, since she well knew the banjo was worth more but had no mind to sell it originally. She'd only grabbed it because it had been sulking in the back corner of an auction house for years. Her boss did regular auctions of the warehouses, and no one wanted the banjo. Fern hadn't paid anything for it.

Truth be told, she might have *paid Chuck* just for the idea.

If a random insurance adjuster wanted something from Fern's stockpile, then others would, too.

So Fern realized exactly what she needed to do to set Stedman out of her head.

She would finally open her antique shop. Nothing big. Nothing life-changing. But she could set up a home base in the parlor. The water leak—and the insurance adjuster—were just the things she needed to kick her in butt. All she had to do was tidy up a bit.

Chapter 15

With new energy, Fern took a quick shower, pulled on a fresh pair of Christmas leggings and a worn t-shirt, blasted "Jingle Bell Rock," and set about a plan.

She had a stack of unused notebooks in the parlor, and she selected a red one to frame things out.

Several internet searches later and about five lined pages filled from top to bottom with lists and brainstorms, she had something to work from. And it would require that she take stock.

And *that* would require that she clean her house. For once, and for all.

It was a painful thought, cleaning. What if she came across something of her mother's that she hadn't before discovered? Would she fall back down the well of nostalgia and heartache?

Toffee rummaged around in the boxes to the side of her desk, clawing excitedly as though she knew what was about to come.

Whatever Fern found, she'd have to deal with. She could do it. If she could muster the strength to call Stedman and *then* invite him for coffee and *then* have dinner with him, she could do anything.

Four empty boxes gawked in the foyer. She would drag her goods to them, categorizing as she went: Sell, Trash, Store, and ?.

Anything that didn't fit into a box would have to go onto the veranda in front. It was cold. Snow encroached on the deck. But weather would not get in the way of her inertia.

Fueled by marshmallow-studded hot cocoa and last year's clearance-rack candy canes, she got down to it.

By lunch, Fern officially had three full boxes. The ? box was not full, but a few items did sit in the bottom, waiting to meet their fate. And, since exhaustion is one way to turn indecision into action, those few trinkets would likely find themselves in the trash before sunset.

Her stomach began to rumble, and despite the fact that she'd warmed up from working, potato soup sounded perfect. Before heading into the kitchen, she stopped off in the front hall bath to quickly surveil what she'd be doing after lunch.

Cinnamon-scented hand soap and a cinnamon-scented candle to match and a hand towel embroidered with a stocking lay neatly at the corners of the sink. All necessities that could stay right where they were.

She popped open the medicine cabinet. First aid supplies. Stacks of plastic-sleeved toothbrushes. She pulled everything out. These were the types of extras that surely would come in handy one day. She couldn't trash them—wasteful— and she couldn't store them—impractical. She had to keep them. Just, somewhere else. Somewhere more orderly.

So, for now, they could rest on the countertop.

Then, she opened the door of the narrow side table that stood adjacent to the pedestal sink. Fern pulled a packaged foursome of toilet paper out to peek at the back. A wooden box, taller than it was wide, sat, hiding in the shadows.

Fern knew exactly what was inside.

It was something she'd hidden from herself years before. As soon as Eleanor died. And then she added to it once Stedman left. The most valuable jewelry in the house sat in that box, protected from dust. Protected from Fern's tears.

A lump formed in her throat. This was just the thing to derail an otherwise perfect day.

So, she left it. Nothing else filled the cabinet. She had no other cause to clean it out.

Fern returned the toilet paper, closed the door, swallowed her lump, and marched to the kitchen. There, she killed the music. When her mother died, Christmas cheer felt morbid. But she overcame that, accepting that everything about the holidays was an homage to Eleanor Monroe.

But when it came to the hard stuff—*Eleanor's belongings*—there was no hope.

"Toffee, are you a potato soup gal or a clam chowder type?" Fern turned her attention idly to the cat as she pulled cans from the pantry and rummaged for the small copper pot she used mainly for soup.

"Actually, I prefer chicken noodle."

Fern whipped around.

Standing in the doorway to her kitchen was that newly nosey neighbor. Maggie.

"You scared the bejeezus out of me!" Fern cried.

Maggie smiled and walked in. "I don't normally barge in, but your front door was wide open, and it started snowing. I hollered for you, but you didn't answer. So then I panicked and thought you might be dead or dying."

The women laughed together, like old friends. It felt great.

"Please, have a seat," Fern offered, grabbing a can of chicken noodle from the back of the pantry. "Is Briar with you?"

Maggie shook her head. "She's with Travis's mom today. I don't care for the woman, but I trust her. I suppose."

Fern didn't understand but didn't ask for clarification either. She simply offered a sympathetic smile and set about heating up the copper pot while washing out a second stainless steel one. A third pot of potpourri bubbled on the back burner.

"Do you work, Maggie?" Fern allowed herself a small question, hoping it didn't come across as rude.

Maggie shook her head and joined Fern at the stove, leaning back onto the counter. "I went to beauty school. Sometimes I do hair in my house, but nothing more. Travis makes enough."

"Like Dolly Parton," Fern answered.

"Hm?"

She explained, "Like Dolly Parton in *Steel Magnolias*. I love that movie."

"Oh yeah, of course. One of my favorites, too. It's so sweet and southern. Sad, too," Maggie agreed, her eyes studying the kitchen.

A thought occurred to Fern. It turned to sentences in her mouth and before she knew it, she was saying it. "I can't imagine losing a child. Sometimes, it makes me feel better to watch movies like that. Where a mother loses a child. I know my mother wouldn't be strong like Sally Fields. I don't know what she would do if she lost me. It was better that she went first." Fern looked up to Maggie, whose expression was unreadable. "I'm sorry. That was a weird thing to say. I—I don't know what I'm talking about."

"No, no. I get it," Maggie answered. "It's a way to make you feel like it's not bad that your mama died. I get it. I don't have a mom, either, you know."

Fern did. She knew well. The two smiled at each other, then Fern remembered her manners. "What would you like to drink with your soup? Water? Sweet tea? Hot cocoa? I mean, I've got the soup right here. You're already inside. Might as well stay for a proper lunch." All previous humiliation and discomfort had melted away.

"I'd love some hot cocoa. As long as you have marshmallows, that is."

"Look around you, Maggie. Is this a house that *wouldn't* have marshmallows?"

Maggie laughed in reply and returned to the table, where Fern deftly served a fat mug of cocoa and a Santa Claus bowl piled high with fresh marshmallows.

"Thanks," Maggie said. "You know, my friend Becky and I came here a couple months back."

Fern sat with her own mug, sipping silently before answering. "I know. I remember. Becky Linden. She wanted to know about Darla."

"That's right," Maggie said. "You and Becky are sort of alike. She appreciates antiquey stuff, too. She's fixing up the old schoolhouse out on Overlook Lane."

Fern knew about this. She admired it. Though she'd turned Becky away, she became curious about the woman's plans. Now, of course, she knew.

"I'm sorry if I was harsh to you and Becky," Fern admitted. "When you came to ask about her, I mean. It's a touchy subject. She and my mother were friends. I've had a hard time getting over my mom's death." Her voice shook and she tried to take a sip to mask the emotion.

Fern expected Maggie to retract. Or perhaps to apologize and fall silent. She expected Maggie to let her cry or awkwardly excuse herself. But the bottle-blonde woman did neither. Instead, she giggled.

"What?" Fern asked, her tears caught in their ducts. "What's so funny?"

"We were scared of you," Maggie revealed, falling into a fit of laughter.

Bewildered, Fern withheld her own smile. "Scared? Of *me*?"

"Yes! You never go to Mally's or the corner market. We don't see you out on a walk. Your house hasn't changed in forever."

Fern interrupted. "You mean I haven't taken down my Christmas decorations in forever."

Maggie nodded as she pulled herself together. "Everyone calls this place *The Christmas House*, you know."

Considering this, Fern was quiet for a minute.

"I'm sorry," Maggie said at last. "I was just trying to lighten the—"

"No," Fern cut in, her eyes growing wide. "I love it."

"You do?" Maggie asked as the soup began to boil.

Fern rose to tend to it and answered nonchalantly over her shoulder. "So people in town know where I am? Where I live? They...*know* about me?

Maggie chuckled. "Well, you're no movie star, but yeah. Everyone knows where The Christmas House is."

This could work in Fern's favor. Having some degree of notoriety. She could leverage it. She could be in on the joke about herself.

"Maggie, I decided I'm starting a shop. I'm cleaning the house, and I'm going to sell antiques. I figured I'd have to rent a storefront on Main or something, but this place is huge. I could do it here. I could make it work right *here*."

Chapter 16

"Okay. But, why now?" Maggie asked.

Fern served the soup and sat, excited and reinvigorated. "Why now what?"

"What made you want to change?" Maggie asked. "I think about that sometimes. What pushes a person to start following their dreams? What pushes them to begin to make the right choices instead of continuin' on making the wrong ones?"

Fern knew there was something more in her question. She considered replying with a question of her own. What did Maggie want in life? But Maggie had come this far, bringing cookies—which Fern still hadn't written a thank-you note for—and now barging in to check on her. She deserved the truth.

And Fern deserved to share the truth. She deserved to have a confidant. So what if they never spoke again? This was her chance to connect with someone other than the ladies at church or the people she worked with. Other than the two people who she wanted to be with but who were no longer available.

"Stedman," she said.

"Who's that?" Maggie replied, scrunching her face then bringing the spoon to her lips. She pursed her lips and blew gently on the broth then sipped it.

Fern studied her. The blonde hair was too yellow. The black eyeliner too black. Fake nails too fake. But if Fern squinted through that, what she saw was someone gorgeous. The girl who might have rivaled a younger Fern, when Fern was the enigma of Hickory Grove. The homeschooled child with white-blonde hair and sparkling eyes.

Maggie had freckles, though they were mostly concealed with makeup. Her lips were full. Smooth. Her eyes clear and bright even behind the black wax. What was she hiding from?

Fern sighed. "My husband."

"Oh, right!" Maggie grew excited. "Okay, you mentioned this when I was here with the cookies. And I thought about it. We *do* remember."

We? "Who's 'we'?" Fern accused.

"Sorry. Beck and I. We're best friends. I had to tell her when you said you were married. That was a big one. You can expect it took me for a shock, you know."

Fern nodded in agreement. "Well, he only lived here for a year or less. We were only married for a year. Exactly one year, in fact."

"*Were* or *are*?" Maggie pried.

"*Are* still. But he left on our wedding anniversary."

Toffee curled around the chairs and hopped up into Fern's lap. An unofficial therapy pet, she knew exactly when her mama needed her. Fern cuddled the furball then set her down to begin on her soup.

Maggie's eyes grew wide. "I'm so sorry," she said. "I can't imagine."

Fern smiled. "Frankly, he's not a bad guy. He was just fed up with me. Truth be told, I didn't even realize it was our anniversary until the next day." She set her spoon down and wiped her mouth with a napkin, staring across the kitchen and taking in all her work in there. An extra cuckoo clock. Two stand mixers.

One cabinet so full that the baking ware was pushing open the door and peeking out from behind.

Maggie followed her gaze and finished the last of her soup. "So that's why you're cleaning your house? To get him back?"

Fern laughed. "No. What I meant was that it all started with him. Well," she paused, frowning, "it actually started with that darn snow storm the evening you were here."

Maggie lifted her eyebrows in surprise then begin to sip her drink.

"I keep my heater low during the day, especially when I'm out of the house, you see. I suppose my laundry room water pipe froze. When I came back, I turned the heater up. The pipe began to thaw and expand. In the middle of the night it burst. I didn't know where the water shut-off valve was. I called Stedman. He came and helped. Then we—" Fern hesitated, unsure whether to share the dinner experience. She glanced up to Maggie whose face was bright. "What?" Fern asked.

"He came over in the middle of the night to help you? Outside? In the snow?"

Fern nodded, understanding where Maggie was going with this. The teenage girl inside her came out to add, "He lives in Louisville, too."

"Fern!" Maggie squealed. "He still loves you. He loves you!"

Fern swatted the idea away. "He still cares about me. Or this house. One of the two. But it's impossible. He said he was going to ask for a divorce, though."

"Weren't you already separated?" Maggie's smile faded into confusion.

"Estranged. For almost four years. Romantically, we are done. Legally, however, I'm still Mrs. Stedman Gale."

"Why didn't you separate? I'm confused." Maggie said, simply.

She wouldn't be able to stand the heartache of a divorce. Fern shook her head. "It's fine. Don't worry about it."

Maggie shook her head. "Girl, you've got to find a way to move on."

"But I am," Fern answered, waving her hand out toward the rest of the house. "I'm going to open a small antique shop. Start selling off the things I've collected."

"That's a neat idea," Maggie agreed. "But it's not enough. You should start dating." Her eyes narrowed on Fern. A severity of expression formed on Maggie's face; she stood and walked closer. "And if you're going to date, then you may as well get a makeover. I'll do it."

Chapter 17

Fern secretly loved the idea, but first she had to make more progress in the house. Maggie, bored apparently, offered to stay and help.

So, together the women worked. Fern giving gentle orders for Maggie to move certain things to certain boxes. Maggie pushing back from time to time.

By the evening, they'd finished sorting the parlor and the great room and had started on the kitchen.

"Briar will be back soon." Maggie sighed and checked her cell phone. "But I can come by tomorrow while she's in preschool, if you'd like?"

Fern smiled, thanked Maggie and said she'd very much like that.

It was incredible how cleaning a house could be a bonding experience for women. Exhausted and now behind in her brokerage work, Fern opted for a quick shower before settling into the sofa with her laptop on her knees, Toffee curled up against her hip, and a new Hallmark Christmas movie glaring in front of her.

The great room was different now. Stark, comparatively. Just furniture and the Christmas decorations were left behind. Gone were junky artifacts and genuine collectors' items that had given the room a shape before.

Fern opened a few tabs on starting an in-home business and turning one's house into a storefront and then took to jotting notes. After she had two full pages worth, she opened her email, bracing for an onslaught of work messages.

Sure enough, fifteen unread messages shouted at her from her inbox, their bold lettering giving her the beginnings of a headache again.

After reaching for a handful of popcorn, she started to click on the first one—a generic message from her supervisor about updating her time sheets.

And that's when she saw it.

An email from *Stedman Gale*.

Fern looked around, suddenly paranoid. Her cheeks flushed. Her pulse quickened. She dumped the popcorn back into the bowl, wiped her hands on her afghan, and—with every ounce of fear shooting to her fingertips—she forced herself to click.

It felt like old times. Like when they first met. Their early interactions were solely through email and chat room private messages. Each notification that Stedman had sent her a message was like a Cupid arrow to her heart. Stedman, admittedly, was her first true romance—childhood movie star crushes never counted, even to a sheltered homeschool girl.

In those days, the correspondence grew increasingly flirtatious. Sometimes even scandalous. She'd taken to purchasing her first laptop so she could write to Stedman in the privacy of her bedroom, away from her mother.

Stedman and Fern's love grew by words. His compliments and pining. Her accepting it and learning from it. She'd turned from awkward young adult into a woman by the time they had met.

And that first meeting was everything she'd hoped it would be. Of course, it was at her house. He came there under her mother's directive. Fern didn't think it was an overprotective thing—for her mother to want to meet Stedman right away. And Stedman was a gentleman about it—anxious to meet Fern's mother, too, in fact.

Fern, unwilling to allow her mother a glimpse into their very first contact, banished the woman to the kitchen while she waited on the veranda in a dark blouse and jeans.

Stedman all but ran up the steps and wrapped her in a hug, whispering into her ear how thrilled he was to meet her. Fern, much to both their surprise, replied with a deep kiss.

The rest of their courtship followed that arc.

They enjoyed a brief engagement, and Fern made the bold choice to move into Stedman's small Louisville apartment.

Being away from her mother was difficult, but being near Stedman was thrilling. During her time there, Fern had taken in all there was to see and do in Louisville, though often alone, since Stedman traveled so regularly.

She liked being alone. Sometimes Eleanor would join her for a day out, and the woman encouraged Fern in her newfound independence.

An intimate wedding ceremony took place in Louisville instead of Hickory Grove. This was Fern's decision. She had always wanted to be married in a theatre, and so they rented out the Actors Theatre of Louisville for one hour.

Stedman's oversized family joined Eleanor Monroe who came alone. The awkwardness and stark differences between the two parties was palpable. But Fern and Stedman didn't care. All that mattered at the time was their love. Their future.

Eleanor gifted the newlyweds with a honeymoon to California. Fern desperately wanted to visit Hollywood, and Stedman was interested, too. Everything seemed perfect.

But before they left, Fern's mother took ill.

A ravenous cancer. Months to live. Inoperable. Untreatable. Hospice care soon.

Without question, the honeymooners gave up the apartment and moved into the house on Pine Tree Lane.

Anyway, it would afford them the chance to eventually find a home to buy for themselves. At the time, Fern thought a miracle might be possible. She clung to Stedman's words of encouragement that *anything could happen*. They even pulled open realtor's magazines between Eleanor's nurse's visits.

Then, when Eleanor's health nosedived, the magazines lay unopened by the front door along with the rest of the mail.

Fern's stress and Stedman's discomfort never seemed to fade. Instead of growing together in those early months, they grew apart. Stedman had come from a great big family. He knew and valued the need to be present and supportive to Eleanor. But his wife's close relationship to her mother and anxiety over her impending death often left him to occupy himself. He didn't seem to mind it. But a new normal had formed. By the time Eleanor passed, the romance between Fern and Stedman felt like little more than a bad omen.

She slept in her mother's room, thwarting Stedman's efforts at taking care of her once the funeral had come and gone.

Any moment Fern had stopped crying and began to seem like herself, Stedman asked if she was ready to move on. He offered distractions and ideas, but it was always too soon.

But now, she *was* ready. Unfortunately, she was also *too late*.

Yet, here was Stedman, sitting in her inbox again. A formal attempt at communication to others. But to her, it was an intimate reminder of how their romance began.

She'd begun to squeeze her eyes shut, but now, as she opened the message, she slowly peered into the screen.

The subject was a simple *Hi*.

"Hi," Fern whispered as her breath caught in her chest.

She read on.

Hi Fern,

I'm sorry to bother you, but is there any chance you still have my watch? The one you gave me...? If so, could I swing by to pick it up? Or we could meet somewhere if you'd prefer. If not, no problem.

Thanks.

Stedman

Chapter 18

Bewildered.

She was utterly bewildered. Just the night before he used the "D" word. Discomfort had replaced familiarity and her mind had swirled with images of him taking other women to dinner. Wooing other women. Maybe ones who liked movies, too.

Fern swallowed hard and drew a hand to her mouth, chewing on a hangnail that wasn't there. Fern never chewed on her nails. It was a bad habit that didn't belong to her.

Was his email pretense? Was it the opposite? An attempt to move on and recommend that she do the same? Should Fern feel sad and angry or hopeful and thrilled?

The watch in question was the one buried with her mother's wedding ring and her own. In the box in the downstairs bath. Behind the toilet paper.

It was the watch she'd given Stedman on their wedding day.

Why in the world would he want it back?

She asked Toffee as much, but Toffee had no answer. The fluff of a cat yawned herself into a stretch, closing her eyes and feigning sleep.

Without Maggie around to advise her, Fern interlaced her fingers, stretched them out dramatically, and took to her keyboard.

Stedman,

I'll look around. Is it urgent? I'm in the middle of a big project.

Fern

***

Fern forced herself to set aside all thoughts of Stedman, going so far as to finish her work emails and close her laptop for the night.

She made it a rule not to add any email apps to her phone, so as long as the laptop was closed, she was safe from a reply.

The next morning, she spent the first couple of hours tending to a few business transactions.

Maggie had mentioned that Briar went to the afternoon session of preschool, and sure enough, at 1:25, Maggie was back. This time bare-faced and in sweats. Snow from beyond the veranda framed her face as did growing stacks of furniture and large items to be donated. All of it overshadowed the decrepit Christmas decorations that remained.

Fern pointed beyond Maggie. "We'll start out here. I'm feeling bold."

"All right," Maggie said as she took in the front porch and yard. "Since it's Christmas, what are you thinking here? Ditch it all and get new stuff?"

Fern's mouth opened in a gasp. "No!" she answered at first. She shook her head and then went on. "I'm sorry. I didn't mean to raise my voice. But, no. A good deal of it can be fixed or tidied or rearranged. I'm certain. Some things might have to go. But all these decorations were my mother's."

A silence fell across them, and Maggie rubbed her arms up and down her sides. "I know it's touchy, Fern. I understand. But, it's also why—" She stopped short, thinking better of what she was going to say.

Fern studied her. "I know. I know it's why I haven't moved on. Why I couldn't right things with Stedman. Or move out. Or keep my job."

"Your job? I thought you worked from home," Maggie answered, stepping closer to Fern and to the warmth coming from inside the house.

"I was a curator at the Dotson in Louisville. For years, actually. I commuted daily. Still did when my mother was dying. I didn't start brokering until Stedman left." Fern closed her eyes for a moment and let out a long breath. There. She'd said it. All there was to say—she said it.

Before she could open her eyes again, she felt Maggie's arms wrap around her.

"I know this is hard, but look at you. You're moving in the right direction. Don't stop now," she whispered into Fern's ear.

Fern nodded, hugged back, and then pushed away. "I'm not a charity case, Maggie. I appreciate your help, but I would never want you to see me as a poor old lady who lives next door."

Maggie laughed. "I've never thought that of you. I thought of you as the scary, weird lady next door."

Fern joined in her laughter and felt herself warm up. "Okay, then let's do it." Just as she began to mark the larger pieces on the porch, a truck pulled up to the curb. Clunky and yellow. Fern stood and blew puffs of frosty air in the direction of the new interloper before glancing up to Maggie, who was tugging down a strand of half-broken Christmas lights from over the front window.

Maggie smiled mischievously at Fern then descended from the patio chair on which she stood, tugged her sweatshirt sleeves over her hands and jogged down the steps and out to the street.

"Who's that?" Fern called after her.

Maggie turned her head as she jogged and replied, "Reinforcements!"

Out of the truck popped a snowsuit-clad woman who could be none other than Becky Linden. Maggie's best friend and Hickory Grove's prodigal daughter, who'd returned to town only recently.

Fern hadn't known Becky any better than she knew Maggie. But she was familiar with the Linden family.

"Hi," Becky beamed as she neared Fern. "It's great to see you, Fern." She opened her arms to hug Fern. Two hugs in one day. It was... nice.

"Hi. Becky, right?" She allowed Becky the embrace and offered a suspicious smile.

"That's right. We were here a couple months ago about your friend. Well, we solved the mystery, you might like to know." The woman prattled on about the circumstances and some unsurprising connection to the abandoned property on Overlook. Finally, she finished her spiel and stood back a step to take in the house.

"Fern," she went on. "I've always loved your house. And I've always loved that you just keep the decorations up. Why shouldn't we be festive all year?" She asked, searching Fern's and Maggie's expressions for validation.

Maggie chuckled and shook her head, but Fern held up a hand. "Actually, that's sort of what I'm thinking, too." She flicked a glance to Maggie who frowned. "No, no. Hear me out. Clean up the decorations we have, toss the junk, and replace with pieces that will age better. Evergreen pieces. And," she paused, watching the women's expressions. Maggie still frowned and now jumped up and down as if to warm herself. Becky watched patiently, a little fire in her eyes.

"Go ahead, Fern," the latter urged her.

"Well, I'm hoping to turn the parlor into an antique shop. Maggie says everyone calls this place The Christmas House, so I'm going to leverage the fame a little. It's risky, but it's a dream of mine. And, I think I'm ready to see it through."

The last time Fern took a risk, she met the man she would marry. The man she loved. The man who, hopefully, would email her back with an apology, a confession. Anything.

"I love it. How can I help?" Becky's optimism was catching.

Maggie smiled behind her and nodded. "Help me with these lights. We can replace them with clear globe string lights. Do you happen to have any, Fern? If you wait until after Christmas, they'll go on sale."

Fern scoffed. "Are you kidding me? I guess our short time together has taught you nothing, Maggie." She gestured to them to follow her down a narrow walk over to her garage, which yawned open, ready for more boxes. Fern pointed to a corner of red bins with green lids. "Christmas," she said.

"Why wouldn't you take those lights down if you have new ones?" Maggie asked, innocently.

Fern shrugged. "Grief. I've had a hard time getting over my mother's death. Christmas reminds me of her. I can't stand the thought of removing something from this house that she touched last."

Maggie and Becky kept quiet.

She smiled back at them. "It's okay. I'm making progress. Lots of progress. Maggie's even giving me a makeover, right Maggie?"

Becky looked over at her friend and grinned. "That's wonderful, Mags."

"Anyway, let's do this. Maggie, I'm ready. If it's broken and we can't fix it—it goes. If it's broken and doesn't match our aesthetic—it goes."

"What if it's not broken and doesn't match our aesthetic?" she answered, seriously.

Fern considered that. "Put it in the question mark box."

Maggie and Becky began to pull the Christmas bins from their tight position in the back corner. Fern returned inside to make some hot cocoa and grab her boombox. It might be thirty years old, but it played Christmas CDs without skipping and would plug into the now-available outlet on the porch.

They sang as they worked. Maggie providing baritone as Fern took tenor and Becky alto. They sang through the classics and stopped occasionally to warm themselves with hot cocoa.

Becky, who'd been living in Tucson for twenty years, had to go in and sit by the fire from time to time. Maggie and Fern laughed at her as if Fern was the third musketeer, always a part of their friendship somehow.

Fern felt like the Grinch at the end of the movie.

Her heart grew three sizes that day.

A few hours later—after Maggie left to get Briar and returned with the nap-ready child—the front was transformed.

They'd moved all the big items that had been inside over to the garage. The lawn ornaments—a cracked Rudolph and the other reindeer, were marked for trashed. The Santa and Mrs. Claus garden gnomes were marked for charity.

It turned out Fern had enough "stock" to replace the now missing decorations. All three women agreed the house just didn't look the same without string lights and greenery. Still, they kept it tasteful. A rope of clear globes lined the eaves under the porch. Maggie, daring girl that she was, had climbed the roof to affix another string under the upper eaves, and she used Fern's dad's old ladder to mount two wreaths beneath the second story windows.

Maggie and Becky egged Fern on to do the honor of adding the third wreath to the fascia above the cupola. Fern was never afraid of heights, but she realized she'd never climbed anything either. It was a silly realization and one Maggie and Becky made of fun her for.

But she liked to be in on a joke about her. After being the absentee butt of jokes for years, she loved taking part and laughed thoroughly at herself.

Once they finished, the three women retired inside. Briar had made herself at home, snuggled up with Toffee on the sofa as cartoons danced across the television screen. Maggie stoked the fire into oblivion while Fern and Becky started a batch of banana bread.

"Briar, you come help us!" Becky called from the kitchen.

Sure enough, the little girl dragged her blanket (Fern's afghan) into the kitchen and managed to get up on a chair and help stir and pour and stir and pour.

After the loaf baking, everyone returned to the television. Fern, Maggie, and Becky with glasses of eggnog. Briar with a vintage tumbler of warm milk and a tray of cookies.

There were a few weeks left until December 25, but for the first time since her mother passed, Fern could feel the spirit of Christmas.

They chatted and laughed together, and Fern got to hear about all the gossip she'd missed out on having been such a hermit for so long. Becky's blossoming relationship. Maggie's failing one. The latter spoke only in gestures above Briar's head until the little girl faded into an all-encompassing sleep.

By the time the banana bread was devoured the eggnog emptied, the four of them called it a night.

Maggie promised to return in a couple days if Fern still needed help. Becky reminded Maggie that she was giving Fern a makeover.

Once everyone was gone and it was just Fern and Toffee, a happiness set in. The kind that only takes hold when a person feels... safe.

Buzzing with energy, she grabbed her laptop and opened her email. Fern had nearly forgotten about the email exchange with Stedman by then.

And so she was shocked when she saw he'd replied.

Chapter 19

Fern,

How does this sound: I can meet you at Mally's. I'll be traveling through Hickory Grove on my way to Corydon tomorrow, if you're free then? My time is sort of flexible so long as it's earlier than two. If you're not busy, maybe we can have coffee? I don't want to bother you, though, so if you can't meet, I can also swing by your house. Or would you rather mail it? Whatever works for you. Just hoping to get the watch, of course.

I look forward to your response!

Stedman :)

***

Fern's heart stopped at the exclamation point and pounded at the smiley face. It was very Stedman. The rambling sentences. The apologetic tone. Well, it was Stedman *pre-marriage*. When he was feeling things out.

When he was flirting with her. Courting her.

Still, the word "divorce" clung to Fern's heart. She couldn't see herself overcoming such a suggestion. If he'd wanted to talk about divorce, why not email her about *that* instead of taking her to dinner?

And, did he hope to hear back soon because he was desperate for his watch or desperate to see her? And if he was desperate to see her, why didn't he come out and say that over dinner instead of recommending they resume a *friendship*.

So many questions.

Before responding, she clicked back to her inbox and skimmed the other emails. Several from work sat waiting. One from Liesl Hart.

Curious, she opened Liesl's message.

Hello, Fern!

I hope you won't mind I pulled your email address from the directory. At our board meeting, one of the gals asked if the Tree Lighting Ceremony would still be held in the traffic circle adjacent to Hickory Grove High. If memory serves, you were working on securing the location back in September or October. I'm sure it's all settled and this email is nothing more than a nuisance.

Will you let me know? Either by responding here or joining us for the auxiliary meeting tonight?

May the spirit of Christmas be with you,

Liesl

Fern grasped at her chest and checked the time stamp on the email and the time on the computer clock. Liesl had sent it at quarter of noon. It was now ten after five. She racked her brain briefly for memory of when these darn monthly meetings took place. Six. Six! She could still go!

But, then. What would she say?

No, the school board had tabled her request to use the traffic circle, directing her instead to the town manager. She went to the town manager and he passed the buck to the town council. By then, she'd missed the council meeting.

She'd been at dinner with Stedman.

Panic filled Fern's gut, and she worried her hands together over and again. Maybe the town manager could assign the permit without the council's permission. Why would they need permission for the tree lighting anyway? It had become a tradition in Hickory Grove. Only two years' worth of tradition, but still, the town seemed to enjoy having a ceremony. The Ladies Auxiliary sure loved it.

Fern considered her options: go to the meeting: reveal that she hadn't quite secured the permit but was fairly certain she still could *OR* skip the meeting, ignore the email and play dead.

Leaning toward playing dead, her mind fell back to Stedman. Stedman who seemed to be giving her a second chance. Stedman who might break her heart all over again.

The tree lighting had nothing to do with him, but it had everything to do with her. This was Fern's moment. Her moment to *come alive*.

After all, she'd been playing dead for years.

***

"There she is!" Liesl's cheery voice trilled through the family room of Little Flock Catholic Church. The usual suspects were in attendance. Five women. Six including Fern.

Fern knew she wasn't late. Was this a coupe? Staged in order to out her as unreliable and useless?

No, it couldn't be. As far as they knew, she was arriving to confirm all was well for the tree lighting ceremony.

And, she was.

"Merry Christmas, ladies," Fern replied, her voice even and assured despite the clench in her chest.

She'd never done anything like she was about to do. She'd never dreamed of doing anything like she was about to do. She'd even set aside her reply to Stedman in order to breathe through the plan as she dressed as sharply as possible in a Christmas sweater and black slacks. She didn't have time to do her hair, so she opted for a quick braid before brushing on a bit of mascara.

As if on cue, Trish Daley commented. "You look nice tonight, Fern."

Fern accepted the compliment with confidence and took her seat in the circle between Trish and Liesl.

"Why don't we begin with a prayer?" Liesl suggested.

The women bowed their heads and clasped their hands.

Liesl went on. "Dear Lord. We would grant that You bless this meeting and these good women with Your spirit tonight and all the year round. May You encourage us to honor Your glory as we take on the job of preparing our community to celebrate Your birth on Christmas Day and share in the spirit of Christmas all the year 'round. In Jesus Christ's name we pray."

"Amen," the group concluded in tandem.

"First order of business. The tree lighting, of course. Fern did you get my email? I hated to bother you but hadn't heard back since our last meeting." Liesl's voice was sugar sweet and lilting.

Fern cleared her throat and shifted on the metal chair under her bottom. "Thank you for the email, Liesl. I was glad to see your name pop into my inbox. A holiday treat, really." Genuine appreciation was still a distance. But if women in Hickory Grove were taught one thing, it was *fake it till you make it.*

Bless their hearts.

Liesl smiled tightly and her eyes flashed along the other members who were either too bored or too tired to care about the game between Liesl and Fern.

She went on. "Ladies, I have disappointing news. Due to—ah—due to municipal red tape, I was unable to secure our spot at the roundabout." Fern paused only long enough for the women to react accordingly, mouths agape. But she went on before anyone could cry out in revolt. "But," Fern said, holding up her hand, "I have a backup plan."

Liesl batted her eyelashes at an unnatural rate and frowned deeply. "Fern, this can't be. Everyone in Hickory Grove—heck, everyone in George County expects us to show up at the traffic circle. Fern, *what happened*?"

Fern thought about that question briefly. Every year, she'd been reliable Fern. Reliably messy. Reliably quiet. Reliably sad, even. And, yet, reliably zealous about setting up the tree lighting ceremony.

But in a couple short weeks, all of that had changed. All of it.

"I'm sorry, Liesl. I'm sorry, ladies." She opened her hands, supplicant. "But please hear me out."

The women nodded, suspicious and politely angry.

Fern glanced at Liesl for permission to reveal her Plan B. Liesl glared, shrugged her shoulders, and dropped her hands from her hips. "Go on, Fern."

"My house."

Trish squinted. "Huh?"

Fern cleared her throat and repeated her idea. "My house. We can have the lighting ceremony at my house."

No one replied, at first. Fern wondered if what she was about to say next would clarify things or confuse them or come out like a joke. But she had no choice.

"I know what everyone calls it. They call it 'The Christmas House.' So, it makes sense. I'm close enough to Main Street so people can park and walk. It's a big property, as you know."

Trisha's squinting softened. Two others began to smile. Liesl flushed crimson, which told Fern that it was a terrific idea.

The Christmas House. Fern was the woman who lived in The Christmas House. She wouldn't accept other people making a joke about her unless she was in on it. It was time for Fern to be *in on it.*

"It's all right," she added, quickly, as she deciphered their curious expressions. "I don't mind. I've actually been working on cleaning things up. A few friends are helping. We're nearly done. Just a little more organizing inside and the place is set."

Liesl and Trish locked eyes and silently exchanged a nod. Annie Fairbanks broke in with a question. "How will we fit everyone in your front yard? That can't work." Annie Fairbanks was new to Hickory Grove. Even more an outsider than Fern in most ways. Just not the ways that counted.

Trish quickly corrected her. "Haven't you seen the Monroe place? It's up on Pine Tree. It's massive. It's more of an, oh, what would you call it? Estate? More of an estate than a house."

Fern blushed.

Annie replied, "Oh *that* house? I didn't know *you* lived there, Fern. The one with the broken decorations? Thought it was abandoned or something."

Liesl, for her part, turned her glare on Annie. "Fern's parents owned the home. Her father passed years back. Her mama just passed a few years ago. Fern's been keeping it up since then, as y'all know."

Fern looked at Liesl, awestruck by the compassion. Her chest burned and she wanted desperately to hug the woman. She didn't. Instead, she lifted her chin and went on. "Thank you, Liesl. We've put up new, clear string lights. Wreaths. If the snow melts, I'll cut back the hedges, but I doubt that'll be an issue in the next couple days. And, since we can't very well transport the fir tree from the roundabout, I figure we can bring in a freshly cut one or we can use my mother's artificial tree."

The women nodded, quiet now. Interested.

"How big is your mama's?" Trish asked.

"Fourteen feet. She bought it for the foyer."

"Foyer?" Annie answered. The woman couldn't fathom it, clearly.

"There's a guest bath off the foyer. I figure I can serve hot cocoa. Everything else will remain the same. It's just the location that will change. And, really, ladies, off Main and Pine Tree is more centralized than up by the high school."

The women nodded, again. Liesl spoke. "I think it's a wonderful idea, Fern. But is it okay to host a public event on private property?"

Fern shrugged. "Since the school district and the town were juggling jurisdiction, I figure we have to work with what we have. In such a short time frame, we have my property. And the tree lighting isn't technically a town event. We are the ones who put it on, after all." She waved around the circle.

The women beamed back. The Little Flock Catholic Ladies Auxiliary had, perhaps, never known such a responsibility. The compliment clearly sealed the deal.

Liesl flashed a broad smile at Fern. A *real* one. "Well, that settles it, I s'pose. The Hickory Grove Tree Lighting will take place at Fern's house."

Trish added, "The Christmas House."

A small applause filled the space, and Fern glowed with pride.

They set about assigning tasks and organizing a game plan.

But by then, Fern's mind returned to Stedman and his email.

Chapter 20

Stedman,

If you'd like, you can come by here. I'll be available most of tomorrow (working from home). Why don't you call me when you leave? I can prepare a snack or lunch depending on the time.

Yours,

Fern

***

She thought long and hard about the "yours," and decided it was okay. She used it in many of her correspondences. And, technically speaking, she was still *his*.

Also, his message was nervous and shaky. Fern had the opportunity to be the cool, calm, collected one. Throwing in a sweet salutation was no big deal.

She closed her laptop, folded the afghan neatly across the back of the sofa, shut off the television, and headed to her bedroom with Toffee in her wake and her cell phone clutched in her hand.

As soon as she crawled beneath the tucked sheet and fluffy duvet, snuggling excitedly into the center of the mattress like a teenager who'd just bumped into the cutest boy in town, her phone vibrated.

Fern's heart pounded. Her nostrils flared. A smile broke out on her mouth in the dark bedroom. The chill in the air evaporated as she grabbed the phone from her nightstand. Toffee mewed irritably.

Sure enough.

Stedman.

And, significantly, he was *calling* rather than *texting*.

She shushed Toffee and twisted in bed so that she could press the phone on her top ear and muffle her bottom ear from the mews.

"Hello?" she whispered involuntarily as if there was a houseful of people who might wake up and overhear a secret.

Stedman's voice was not a whisper, and he seemed to be talking through great noise as though he were at a party or the like. "Fern?"

She let out a breath she didn't know she was holding. "Yes. Stedman?"

He laughed. "Hey, Fern. Hope I didn't wake you up." His Louisville drawl curled thickly through the receiver. It transported Fern to one of their best dates: a tour of the Maker's Mark distillery. Stedman had talked to the tour guides like he ran the place. His smooth southern voice adding an authority to his knowledge on bourbon whiskey and all things Kentucky.

Antiques were to Fern what bootlegged beverages were to Stedman.

The clock on her bed stand glowed. It was nearly nine o'clock. She *could* have been asleep. "It's a little late, but I'm not asleep. I was just lying down to... to rest." She squeezed her eyes and shook her head. "Well, I was about to go to bed, yes. Long day." *Hush up, Fern.*

"Oh, I could shoot you a text instead? Or call in the morning?" he asked, his voice eager and the background noise gone. *Where was he?*

"What are you doing right now?" She bit down hard on her lower lip, stilling herself for the answer. *He was in Hickory Grove! At Mally's! Waiting there until he got the green light to head her way.*

Wishful thinking.

"I'm out for drinks with friends," he answered. "Your email came through on my phone, so I stepped out. Are you sure you don't want me to call back tomorrow? I guess I could have waited."

She swallowed, her heartbeat softening. Toffee had fallen back to sleep and was purring against Fern's thighs. "No, we can make plans now. What time did you want to swing by?"

"Well," he began before clearing his voice. "Honestly, I can come by at any time. My meeting in Corydon was canceled. I'm all yours."

She knew it.

Again, Fern's pulse throbbed. "All right. Well, a few friends are coming over to help me set up for something. I need to see when they'll be by." It was all true, but it came rolling out of her mouth like a series of fibs crafted to impress him. She didn't want him to think she was trying to impress him. She wasn't even sure she *wanted to impress him*. She just wanted to be herself. Fern wanted Stedman to see her as she really was. As she always was.

"You can send me a message and tell me when to come by. How's that?"

"That's great," she answered.

Stedman's voice lowered an octave. "You sound different," he said.

Confused, she tried to clear her throat a little. "I'm the same old me." Fern smiled to herself as she said it.

"You sound... *happy*," he replied, almost accusatory.

She blinked in the dark room. Fern hadn't stopped to think about her own happiness. Who does, anyway? Whoever stops and thinks, *I'm so happy! Oh, my. I'm feeling happy!* Fern never did. She opened her mouth to reply, but Stedman went on.

"*Are* you happy? Sorry. Wasn't tryin' to... ah. I don't know. Wasn't tryin' to pry. Sorry. You just sound different. Happier. I know dinner didn't end well, but—" he trailed off.

"I am, actually. I am happy," she answered, sighing lightly into her phone.

Fern closed her eyes for a moment and pretended that Stedman wasn't on the phone. She pretended he was in bed next to her, lying on his side as she tucked herself along his torso. She imagined they'd just finished watching *White Christmas* and he'd helped her rinse out their hot cocoa mugs before settling in for a long winter's nap. *Are you happy, Fern?* He'd whisper down to her. *I am happy*, she'd replied before shutting her eyes and dozing off.

An unfamiliar voice came screeching on the other end of the line.

Confused, Fern opened her eyes in the dark, pulled the phone away from her ear, looked at it, returned it to her ear, then said, "Stedman?"

A commotion seemed to ensue and Fern listened on as Stedman convinced someone he'd be back in a moment.

"Fern, I have to go. I'll call in the morning, okay?"

Gone was his deep drawl.

Tears came out of nowhere, stinging her eyes and taking her wholly by surprise. She would have said goodbye.

If not for the other voice. The voice nagging Stedman to come back.

The woman's voice.

Chapter 21

Two in the morning rolled around, and Fern gave up on sleep. She dragged herself from the bed, tossed the covers over Toffee's warm little body, and trudged downstairs into the great room.

The fire was long dead. She'd tried to get one started before settling down to check her email but had failed. Now it offered only cold air and a log with black edges beneath which she'd wedged burning chunks of newspaper.

The new string lights shone outside the wide bay window which now lay bare and exposed. She felt naked in this cleared-out, barren space and wondered if she ought to turn the lights off now.

The thought of walking from the sofa to the light switch in the foyer suddenly felt overwhelming, so instead Fern clicked on the television set and perused until she stumbled across *A Charlie Brown Christmas* playing on repeat for the next three hours. She tuned in and checked out, wrapping herself in the thick afghan that her grandmother Monroe had probably spent weeks—maybe months—crocheting. A woman whose hands were delicate and frail but who got up each day to finish any number of projects. A woman who saw things through.

A woman quite unlike her very own granddaughter.

Unable to focus on the show, Fern allowed herself to rest her eyes.

Before she knew it, the glow of the Christmas lights became washed out by early morning sun. At some point, Toffee must have joined her, because when she stirred awake, she could feel the low purr vibrating against her abdomen. She smoothed her hand along Toffee's Persian fur and promised breakfast if the little thing would get up with her. It was no use. Maybe Toffee was depressed, Fern thought. What cat preferred sleep over Fancy Feast?

After her own breakfast of toast and coffee, Fern gnawed on an old candy cane and stared through the bay window at her front yard. The Ladies Auxiliary would be by this afternoon to assess the space and figure out how they could help Fern set up. Fern didn't need their help, but she had to admit she was excited for them to see her progress.

Nine o'clock rolled around, and Fern had finished a little brokerage work, cleared her inbox, and drawn out a to-do list and a shopping list.

The tree lighting would promise confections, baked goods and warm beverages along with seating areas and music. In the past, it had doubled as a bake sale. The proceeds would go to Women and Children's House, a safe home for abused women in George County.

Fern had a lot to do and only one day to do it. The lighting ceremony was Friday, after all.

She peeked out the window and up the street toward Maggie's home, wondering how they managed to afford a house on Pine Tree Lane.

Then again, Travis seemed scrappy. Plus, his was the only garage in town. Fern sighed on behalf of her friend and then saw Maggie emerge at the bottom of her drive. If they weren't careful, this might just become a routine. Daily neighbor visits. A sad grin took hold of Fern's cramped features and she pulled her sweater more closely around her body.

"Hey girl," Maggie said as Fern opened the front door and ushered her inside. "What room are we tackling today?"

"All that's left is the upstairs, but we have to leave that for now. Are you willing to help me with a different project?"

Maggie shrugged in reply and peered past Fern curiously. "Sure. You have me for two hours today. I'm taking the kids Christmas shopping in Louisville now that they're on winter break."

"Oh, no problem!" Fern's voice was an octave too high. She gestured back to the door. "You know, Maggie, you've already done so much. You really don't need to come over every day now. I know I owe you for your help. Really, thank you. Please don't feel obligated to stay. You should spend time with your family." She looked frantically at Maggie and caught the reddish roots that had been growing out for some days now. Her clean face and sweatshirt and sweats belied a lazy morning. She looked utterly unlike herself. Fern wanted to point it out, but a new tension gripped her.

"I love coming here," Maggie answered blankly. "I mean, I love being with my kids, too. But I really like coming here. And we aren't done with your house *or* with you, my dear friend." She shook a finger at Fern playfully, and the tension burst.

"Well, if that's the case, then I have an idea," Fern replied, smiling. "I went a little mad and offered to host the town tree lighting ceremony here, on the front property, and now I need to set up seating areas. Some of the men will truck the most of the set-up over later today, but I have some folding tables and chairs I'd like to pull up from the basement, clean, and get prepped."

"*You* are hosting the tree lighting? *Here*?" Maggie's mouth stood ajar. Fern nodded. "That's so perfect, Fern! The Christmas House! Of course!" Maggie pointed to the kitchen. "Can I get a hot cocoa before we start?"

"Always," Fern answered.

The two women went to the kitchen and Fern set about warming milk on the stove. Maggie rummaged through the pantry for the cocoa powder and marshmallows then stopped at the cabinet where the thermoses were kept.

"Grab a few more. I haven't told you my idea yet. Well, it's more of a favor than an idea," Fern admitted as she poured more milk into the kettle and set the burner on low.

The warmth was welcome, and Fern felt life returning to her. If she could throw herself into this tree lighting ceremony, then Stedman and his vibrant social life wouldn't matter anymore. They could be friends. Just like they'd agreed at dinner. Friends. Nothing more. Nothing less. A clean divorce. He could go out with his friends and have fun and she could go to bed early and get quality sleep. Simple as that.

"Oh?" Maggie answered, popping a couple marshmallows in her mouth.

"Would your kids like to make a little money?" Fern asked, nervous.

Maggie didn't hesitate. "They'd love to. It's perfect. What do you have in mind?"

"Whatever they are willing to do. Shovel the edges of the drive to clean it up. Haul my Christmas tree out and start decorating it. Maybe Briar could work on a little snowman by the front deck? I need to get this place more decked out than ever." Fern held her breath. She didn't know children. She had no clue if the modern child still did things like chores or enjoyed helping neighbors or had the drive to do a little hard work.

Maggie frowned and waved something off. "Easy," she replied. "They'll *love* it."

And like that, everything was in motion.

Briar made an attempt at a snow angel as the three older ones set about doing exactly what Fern asked of them. An hour in, things were taking shape. Fern had scrubbed the front hall bathroom as Maggie set about entry decor. She had a lot to work with, and used nearly everything.

Fern joined her to admire the styling.

Two miniature artificial trees stood sentinels on either side of the door. Beneath them, sort of spilling down the porch steps were Christmas odds and ends, placed just so. The silhouette of a Santa Claus and Mrs. Claus. A basket full of pinecones tied neatly at the handle with a velveteen red ribbon. Garland curled around the railing. Maggie even found a Christmas doormat Fern had purchased on clearance. The image of a sled and sleigh bells welcomed them inside as they assessed the interior and set about following Maggie's "aesthetic," as she continued to call it.

Maggie made use of a lot of what Fern already had on hand, filling a glass vase with more pinecones and topping it off with a sprig of holly. Fern brought in tall, round, red candles and propped them on round ceramic bases to create a centerpiece on the foyer side table.

"Hang on," Maggie instructed, heading back to the garage for a new trip to the Christmas bins. She returned with yet another string of clear lights—these ones the tiny, pointy kind that usually danced across the boughs of a Christmas tree. "Grab another vase," she directed.

Fern complied and returned with an oversized, antique vase that had belonged to Aunt Irma. Maggie wadded the lights up inside and carefully pulled and played with the set-up on the table until she'd successfully hidden the cord and tucked it behind, stringing it down to the outlet. The result was a bowlful of twinkles. Like magic.

"You are good at this," Fern said, in awe.

"I like to make things pretty, what can I say?" Maggie smiled, satisfied with herself. "Oh, wait. There was one more thing I found I want to add up there." She pointed to the archway that led toward the great room.

Fern frowned. "What?"

"Be right back," Maggie answered, leaving again and then returning with Kai and a step ladder Fern didn't know she had. Kai mounted the ladder and followed his mother's directions as she passed him a screw hook.

On it, he hung a beautiful, robust set of mistletoe. Having done his job and being totally uninterested in this matter, Kai left to return to his snowball fight in the front.

Fern's face fell.

"What? What's wrong? Mistletoe is crucial," Maggie pressed.

Fern shook her head. "I know, it's just. I—I spoke to Stedman. I've *been* speaking to Stedman," she admitted.

Maggie's eyes widened and her head crooked to the left. "What? Tell me everything!"

And so Fern did. She told Maggie everything. The dinner. The emails. The watch. The hope for a reunion. And then, that she was wrong. No love was left. A divorce was inevitable. Friendship was fine. Romance was dead.

Full of the vim and vigor of a diehard teenage friend, Maggie flew into a diatribe against men and especially Stedman Gale.

It was impressive really. And then, concerning. And then, affirming. Maggie was right. It had to end. Women couldn't give into men like Stedman who hadn't the first clue how to treat a lady.

"But he did come help with the water," Fern broke in, unsure why she was defending him.

"Doesn't matter. He said he was going to ask for a divorce, right? And he basically hung up on you, right?"

Fern nodded slowly, uncertain. He didn't quite hang up. And maybe it was harmless. A friend who needed help. Maybe he was helping someone. He seemed to be doing a lot of that lately.

"You know what I think?" Maggie asked, crossing her arms.

"No. What?" Fern blew out a sigh and pushed her sweater sleeves to her elbows, exasperated by herself for even giving Stedman so much as a passing thought. What was wrong with her that she couldn't move on from him? She'd made progress in every other aspect of her life, after all.

"I think you should beat him to the punch," Maggie replied.

Fern frowned. "What do you mean?

"Fern, just do it, already. File for divorce."

Chapter 22

Maggie's kids had finished their jobs and the snowball fight came to a predictable conclusion, with two of them crying and one of them sitting smugly on the front stoop.

After a rambling lecture about taking things too far, Maggie sent them all home.

Fern felt bad for the hardworking kids but understood her friend's irritation. She'd once read the stress levels for parents spiked during the holidays. Though Fern wasn't a parent, she felt the other end. The distinct lack of stress. She wished she had a big family to yell at right about now. Though she and Stedman hadn't enjoyed a fruitful marriage, Fern had often daydreamed that they would at least share in the upbringing of another creature. Maybe rescue a second cat. A dog. Stedman liked birds. And with his oversized family—half a dozen siblings and a few dozen cousins, she could become a generous (if wacky) aunt, hosting her nieces and nephews for weekend sleepovers with movies and popcorn and cuddles.

It never happened.

It never would happen.

Because Fern agreed with Maggie. She could handle the nothingness from the intervening years. She couldn't handle the teasing.

Once Maggie's kids took off toward their house with the promise of payment from Fern in the form of cookies, she stood with Maggie on her front porch and looked out onto the expansive front yard. Less a yard. More a manor, especially now.

Eleanor's too-big tree fit perfectly in the chunky snow, equidistant from the road and her front steps. The kids did a good job of staging little seating areas with her Adirondack chairs off to the far corners. A folding table with two folding chairs stood in the drive, on level ground. Perfect for the hot cocoa bar where she'd also serve cookies and candy canes. The table would need a tablecloth, of which Fern had an ample supply. Maybe the one she'd used the year her mother passed. The one with holly berries and mistletoe.

"Come on, let's get the view from the street," Maggie suggested, tugging Fern down the steps and along the walk. They cut down the drive and toward the mailbox. The walk from the street was exactly ninety-four yards. Stedman had measured it one time, taking in the grandeur of the place when he and Fern had just married. She shook the thought and stared with Maggie.

It was almost perfect. Ornaments and tinsel gleamed from the full boughs of the tree. Each seating area appeared comfortable and provided plenty of space for the event's attendees to sit and relax.

She could envision the hot cocoa bar, where people would stand, puffing cold air to each other in the chilly night as her house glowed with life it had never known.

"It's missing something," Fern complained.

Maggie shook her head. "No way. It's perfect. Anything else, and you'd be *The Christmas House*. Like this, it's simply The Christmas House." Her emphasis on the former title pushed Fern to smile and roll her eyes.

Silence crept back between them.

"I have to go get the kids ready for shopping," Maggie said, her voice low as she rubbed her hands up and down her arms.

Fern nodded. "Yes. I know." She turned to Maggie. "Thank you. Thank you so much, Maggie. For everything."

A breeze cut up the street and blew blonde wisps across Fern's face. She wondered if Maggie was still interested in helping her with a makeover. She felt like she needed it now more than ever.

Fern's future swirled around her.

The tree lighting ceremony would be bizarre. Strangers milling about her front yard, whispering no doubt.

Christmas would be barely different than Thanksgiving—working the community dinner at the rec hall with whoever of the auxiliary ladies had agreed to commit to that one. Whose ever turn it was. Not Liesl's. She already did her stint. Maybe Trish would join Fern.

And then Fern would return here. To a veritable Christmas town rather than a Christmas house. Alone. Little more than hot cocoa and movies to keep her tears at bay. Toffee, suddenly, didn't feel like enough anymore.

Her eyes bubbled up with tears.

"Fern, what's wrong?" Maggie turned to her and rested a red-knuckled hand on Fern's arm.

She shook her head. "The wind just—it's stinging my eyes." She looked up to a bright blue sky. "It'd be nice if a new storm came in. Gave us a fresh blanket of snow."

Maggie looked up, too. "It's clear today, but I think the forecast shows snow tomorrow." She dropped her hand. "You sure you're okay, hon?"

Fern swallowed. Holding the tears in was no use. "The divorce. I'm just upset," she choked out before water spilled out of her eyes.

"Aw. It's okay." Maggie wrapped Fern in a hug and rocked her back and forth on top of the icy street. Fern cried in her new friend's arms at the thought of her old husband. Her dead mother. Her lonely life.

"I think I'm going to call a lawyer today. Get things rolling with it."

Maggie snorted. "You don't need a lawyer." She crunched down on the last sliver of her candy cane. "You can print the paperwork from the web. As long as you don't need alimony or child support, that is."

"How do you know I can get it online?" Fern asked, genuinely curious.

Maggie stared back, white crumbs of the hard candy poking out from the corners of her mouth. "I've looked it up myself."

***

Maggie had left to shop with her kids, and Fern sat on the sofa with a neat stack of freshly printed legalese. The steam from her coffee had long slipped away, finding a path up the soot-stained chimney and out into the late-morning sky. Toffee mewed discontentedly on the floor beside the sofa. Fern knew she wanted lunch. Early. As always. But Fern's own appetite was such that she couldn't deal with her cat or anything else in the world.

This was soon to be her second tragic Christmas. At least Stedman wasn't dying or dead.

Her eyes skimmed the pages, taking in the finality of the contract. It was all very basic, actually. Gentle, even. She might as well be filling out a job application. Position? Ex-wife.

She was just about finished filling in the tiny boxes when the doorbell rang.

Fern's eyes flitted to the bay windows. That morning, Maggie had helped her hang two sets of heavy lace drapes where the blackout curtains lived before the big clean up. Though lighter, she still couldn't see who was standing at the front door. Unwilling to leave the papers in prime Toffee territory, she carried them with her to answer it.

Standing there, with his hands tucked deeply in his coat pockets, a boyish grin splashed across a five o'clock shadow, was her husband.

Chapter 23

"Fern, hey," he drawled as she opened the door and pressed the papers discreetly at her hip. "This place looks amazing, wow. I guess you *have* been busy." His smooth grin faded when she crossed her arms over her chest.

"I didn't realize you still planned to drop by," Fern answered, her face impassive, her heart confused yet again.

He sniffled and rubbed a hand over his mouth. "I'm real sorry about getting off the phone so fast last night."

She met his gaze and faltered slightly before offering him a phony reply. "Oh, no. No. It's fine, really. I should have expected you would be..." again she stumbled, nervous and unsure what, exactly, she meant to say.

Having overheard the awkward interaction, Toffee strolled over and twisted herself through Fern's legs, protective at first. Then she noticed Stedman and all but pounced on his boots like a puppy.

Fern smirked at the overt and uncommon show of affection from an otherwise typical cat. Stedman chuckled and knelt to give Toffee a rub-down.

Having little other choice, Fern said, "Well, come in, I suppose. I don't want Toffee to freeze to death out there."

The excuse was lame, but Stedman seemed to welcome it, whisking the cat off her paws and carrying her into the foyer. Fern knew better than to bring him into the great room with its cozy sofa and frigid fireplace. The kitchen would be more appropriate. Plus, she would have somewhere to set the paperwork, either squarely in front of him or inconspicuously shoved into a drawer.

"I tried calling your cell before I drove up," he said as he set Toffee on a bar stool. "I hope I'm not bugging you?"

Fern answered honestly, "Oh, I've had people over this morning. We've been busy." She tried for a mysterious—even scandalous—effect and it worked.

Stedman lifted an eyebrow. "Oh? I hope...ah...I hope I'm not interrupting something." His eyebrows furrowed and he peered through the kitchen door as if he could see down the hall, up the stairs, and directly into her bedroom.

At such an overt display of alpha-male protectiveness, Fern felt like she could laugh or swoon. Instead, she flushed. "No, they're gone now," she confessed, considering whether to offer more details.

"Oh." Stedman relaxed and eased his body against the island. "Well, I only stopped by for the watch."

Fern's gut clenched at that and her knuckles grew white. Maybe now was the time. If he only came to get an "asset," then what better transition did she need?

"Oh, okay," she replied, involuntarily setting the paperwork on the counter not three feet away from him.

She started to walk past him to go and retrieve the watch, but as she did, he grabbed her wrist.

Fern's head whipped up and back, at him.

Stedman stared at her harder than he ever had.

Warmth crawled up her neck and into her cheeks. She swallowed, becoming aware of herself.

She'd changed very little since Stedman had left. Her hair was still long and light. Her eyes still blue. Her lips still full, much like her hips and bosom. But her figure had largely gone unchanged, and she miraculously continued to enjoy a slight waist and shapely legs despite age, gravity, and any other number of factors. In that moment, she became aware of her body as though she'd previously been nothing more than a ghost, like Marley from *A Christmas Carol*, floating in and out of the house where he'd lived before.

Stedman, too, seemed to become aware of her body. In an instant, he pulled her into him, his arms wrapped around her, his face buried in her neck. Fern was utterly swept away. She grabbed the back of his head in one hand and squeezed her other arm around his shoulders.

He lifted his head and whispered into her ear, "I've wanted to hold you for four years."

Time stopped, and of all the things she could have said—that she loved him, that she missed him, that she wanted to hold him, too—instead, it was the thing from the night before. The suspicion.

The insecurity. Ever present. Ever intrusive.

"Stedman, who were you with last night?"

He stiffened and pushed away, pinning his gaze on her. She watched his Adam's apple bob below his square jawline and nearly regretted breaking the moment.

"Why don't we sit and talk?" he suggested, releasing her now and scratching the back of his head.

She blinked. "Okay."

They moved quietly to the living room, where the tension tripled. A draft cut in, and Fern offered to turn up the heat.

Stedman pointed to a neat stack of firewood next to the hearth. "Somebody has been here, huh?" It was a playful accusation, one that added to the heat between them.

Fern nodded. "Yes, but it's not what you think. My friends are helping set up for the town Christmas tree lighting. We're hosting it here. Tomorrow, in fact. The neighbor kids brought over some chopped wood and stacked it for me." She winced at her missed opportunity to make him as jealous as she felt.

Then again, she was half way to fifty. The games had to stop. She knew this.

"Can I start a fire?" he asked, rubbing his hands together. "It's chilly in here."

"Will you be here much longer?" Fern answered, putting it back on him.

With that, he deftly pulled logs and positioned them just so, adding kindling beneath and setting it aflame before finally rising from the hearth and clapping his hands on his jeans. Then, with purpose and style, he pulled his coat off and tossed it onto the rocking chair.

Like he lived there or something.

"Sharon," he said, sitting on the edge of the hearth, his elbows on his knees.

Fern lowered herself onto the sofa. "Sharon?" she answered, her heart beating in her throat, still.

"You asked who I was with last night. Sharon. And Megan, Dave, Jerry, and Tim."

Quick math eluded Fern as she tried to think through the numbers of his group. The pairs. The design. There was always design in social groups. The leader. The couple. The try-hard. The tomboy woman who claimed to have no interest in anyone, least of all her male friends who were always and ever "just friends." The man in the group who had something else going on outside of the group. A different life that left him aloof and unreliable when it came to tailgate parties and bar crawls.

When they were married, Fern came to know Megan, Dave, and Tim. Megan and Dave were the original married couple. Comfortable. Trusting. Fun-having but always together.

Tim was a try-hard, but a lovable one. He tried to make jokes. He tried to hit on women. He tried to be good at all the things the others were. Often, he failed and the result was comedic. Fern liked Tim. She liked Megan and Dave, too.

Sharon? Jerry? New people. And Stedman split them apart in his list. So, who was who now? In this new social circle?

Toffee found her way to the sofa and cuddled deep into the corner behind Fern. Feline fortitude. "How are Megan and Dave? How's Tim?"

Stedman waved a hand. "Same old, same old. They're doing well." He paused, waiting for her to prompt him again.

She did. "And Sharon? Jerry? Are they another couple?"

It was a softball. He could knock it out of the park if he wanted to. Fib himself into a tryst with his estranged wife then take off into the winter, watch in hand, never to be heard from again. Maybe it wouldn't even be a fib. But it wouldn't matter. All he had to say was *yes*."

"No."

Fern froze. Stedman met her stare. Guilt shadowed his face. She waited for an explanation. When none came, she found her voice. "Are you...*seeing* her?"

His answer came quickly, like a flash flood. "No." He swallowed and stood, nearing the sofa slowly. Fern could smell him. His shampoo. His aftershave. His masculinity. She scooted away, nearly backing into Toffee's warm little body. Stedman sat near her.

"I'm confused," Fern went on. "Who is Sharon?"

"My cousin," he answered, a mischievous smile breaking out across his face.

Fern frowned and shook her head. "I never met any Sharon," she said.

"You did. She was married at the time. She went by Shari. Remember? Shari? Now she's divorced. Goes by Sharon these days. She's trying to get back out there, you know. I guess Sharon is more mature-sounding. And Jerry is a new friend." His voice evened out, but still Fern sensed he was holding back.

She kicked herself for not paying better attention during introductions at the wedding. She kicked herself for being all-consumed with the ceremony. She kicked herself for ignoring what had always mattered to Stedman.

Family.

"You came for your watch, then," she said, starting to rise, embarrassment filling her chest as she realized exactly how she must seem. Like a jealous twit.

He nodded. "Right. I've missed it. I guess I feel naked without it," he answered, laughing lightly.

Stedman the optimist. The happy-go-lucky, smooth-talking, social butterfly. Nothing bothered him. Nothing affected him. He was bouncing back. Had been for years.

All he needed was his watch. Then, he'd be on his merry way.

"How come you didn't buy a new one? It's been four years." As if she had to state the obvious.

He shrugged. "Honestly, Fern? I almost did." A serious expression filled his face, and Fern lowered herself back to the couch, her heart pounding in her chest.

Stedman continued, "Four years is a long time to go without it. I'd be lying if I didn't tell you I considered shopping around. I mean, I almost called to get a refund so I could start fresh. I wondered about that dang watch all the dang time, Fern."

Shopping around? Fern felt rage rise inside of her. "If you wanted your watch so badly, why didn't you come back? Why didn't you call? Or send a letter? Instead, you wait until we go out for *dinner*? And tell me you were planning to ask for a divorce? What is this, Stedman?" Her hands flailed about her house. Everything in it was unfamiliar, save for a snoring cat.

He closed his eyes for a moment and opened them again. "Our relationship began with communication, Fern. Our chats. Our emails. Our phone calls and then dates. We were good at talking. We *knew* each other. And then, you weren't there. There was no communication. All you cared about was your mom. I'm sorry, Fern. I'm sorry she died, and I'm sorry I left, but could you blame me? I was living in your mother's house with a woman who didn't want to be a wife. We could have dealt with that, but you didn't want to talk to me anymore. I saw a long road, I admit. I saw a future where I'd have to beg you to move on, and I wasn't up to the task. But could you blame me?" He ran his hands down his thighs, looked around himself at her house—*their* house—and stood. "Listen, I should go. I don't need the watch. I just needed you to know that despite it all, I never stopped loving you." He ran his hands down his thighs.

Fern joined him, unsteady on her feet. "Stedman, I'm sorry, too. And, I never stopped loving you, either. I still love you. Today. Now. I love you."

Blood pounded in her ears and her skin prickled up her spine and into the nape of her neck as Stedman strode from the fireplace, slid his arms around her waist, and pressed his mouth onto hers.

She felt like a movie star in a classic film, her blonde hair blown back by some manly force that was invisible to the viewers in the movie theatre. Her slight jaw working opposite his while their lips and tongues moved in perfect rhythm.

His kiss was new and wholly unfamiliar. Four years felt like it might as well be a lifetime. Because she did not know this man.

She did not know this passion. And she did not know such a passion with this man.

Toffee mewed behind them, breaking the moment and pushing them to confront each other. Pushing them to *talk*.

"*Wow*," Stedman whispered, running a hand through his hair as Fern smoothed her shirt and rubbed a finger across her lips.

A giggle escaped her lips.

"Fern," he said, tucking his hands into his back pockets. "Maybe—" Cutting Stedman off was the doorbell. They both looked over toward the foyer in surprise. "Oh," he said. "Who could that be?"

She rolled her eyes at him, appreciating that he knew the *old* Fern. Not the *new* Fern. "I'm not entirely sure," she admitted, again rubbing her lips as if to wipe away salacious evidence.

She went to the door and he followed, his chest puffed as though he were, once again, the man of the house.

Maybe he was.

When they passed under the archway that separated the great room from the foyer, Fern glanced up and pointed a slender finger above. Stedman followed her gaze, caught sight of the mistletoe and then reached for her waist, goosing her like they were teenagers. Fern suppressed a squeal in time to see through the windows that it was Liesl and Trisha. She slapped a hand to her head in realization and then gave a pleading look to Stedman.

"The gals from church. We're getting ready for tomorrow's event," she whispered frantically to him, aware of how his presence would seem: confusing at best, scandalous at worst.

Stedman took the hint and bowed before following her through to the foyer.

"Go make yourself at home," Fern hissed. "Coffee's still on." She pointed him away, smoothed her shirt for the second time, and stepped to the door. When she opened it, the women seemed oblivious to anything untoward.

"Fern, hi!" Liesl stood erect, smiling brightly.

Trish chimed in, too. "Fern, oh my!" She waved her gloved hand behind her at the property. "I don't think I've ever been up here. At least not properly," she added, for good, southern measure.

Liesl nodded emphatically and tried peeking around Fern to get a better look inside.

Suppressing the pseudo-guilty secret in her kitchen, Fern answered tightly. "I've been working hard. Getting things cleaned up. Lots going on in my life right now," she said.

The women nodded.

"Why don't you two come in and sit for a moment while I go get us some hot cocoa before we talk shop?" She hoped that Stedman would keep quiet in the kitchen, but if he did make a noise, Fern would simply introduce him.

He was, after all, her *husband.*

For the time being, however, Liesl and Trish could sit in the great room and silently judge all that Fern had accomplished while she went to the kitchen to explain the predicament to Stedman and reminded him he'd simply have to stay until they left. Otherwise, the presence and then absence of his truck might arouse suspicion. Something Fern could do without as she put together her house for a very public event.

But when Fern stepped into the kitchen, all her visions of keeping him secret and then later returning to where they'd left off, melted like a snowball on fire.

Stedman stood at the bar, his face drawn, her completed divorce paperwork in his hands.

Chapter 24

"What is this?" Stedman asked, his voice too loud.

Fern swallowed and looked behind her toward the great room. "Stedman, I—"

He folded the papers and held them tightly in both hands. "No, no. I get it. You were worried I moved on. Meanwhile, *you've* moved on, Fern. Your clean house. Your new friends. This." he slapped the packet on the table and walking backwards, away from her.

"Stedman, wait. That isn't fair," she answered, her eyes darting back again toward the great room. She bit down on her lower lip, stress consuming her at the reality that she'd have to manage both the ladies and Stedman.

More than that, she was panicking. Here she had the opportunity to fix her past, and she had inadvertently squandered it.

Damn Maggie, she thought as she followed Stedman to the hall. "Please, don't go, Stedman," she called after him as he stalled in the entryway.

"Fern, you have company. Let's just... let's just discuss this later, okay?" His face had softened, but he turned away.

"Your watch?" she said, desperate to anchor him in the house. Desperate to prevent him from leaving forever, again, despite her continual insecurities. Her continual bad choices as a wife.

He stopped, midstride. Then turned. "You filled out several pages of divorce paperwork, Fern. Then I show up, and you...you *kiss* me? Without saying a thing? I'm confused.

I'm...confused. Keep the watch. Go deal with the church ladies. Go tend to your new life."

And, with that, he left.

Fern pressed a hand to her mouth, the warmth from his lips was long gone. Her heart was empty once again.

Liesl and Trish appeared at the far end of the foyer and watched in awe as Stedman bowed his head to them, muttered something, and let himself out.

Fern ignored the women and watched him leave. The door opened and closed, a gust of fresh, frigid air blowing in behind him.

***

"Maggie?" she hissed into the receiver. "He was here. We kissed. It was going well, Maggie. I had filled out the papers. He saw them. He left." Her sentences were choppy and nonsensical, but her friend caught the gist and promised to come right over.

Gretchen was in tow. Becky had agreed to babysit the kids.

Maggie's answer was to strong arm Fern into the makeover she no longer wanted. Or needed.

"I don't know how else to apologize for what I've done," Maggie said, as she barged in with a canvas tote and Gretchen texting on her phone in her wake.

Fern felt more despondent than ever.

Liesl and Trish figured out who Stedman was. And, they put the pieces together. Fern tried to recover by giving them a brief tour and rundown of the plan, admitting she'd fallen behind on baking but asserting that everything else was in place.

The women praised her efforts and promised to arrive first thing with the portable heat lamps and remainder of the chairs. The forecast called for snow, and they were incredibly late advertising the new location, but Liesl assured Fern that things would fall into place.

When Fern finished her review of the preceding events to Maggie and a vaguely interested Gretchen, Maggie laughed. "Liesl Hart is a caricature of a small-town gossip. She would do well to let loose and go out dancing. She can pull the reindeer antler out of her rear while she's at it."

Gretchen snorted at her mother's callous joke then returned to organizing bottles and tubes, bowls, and foil squares.

"Thanks, Gretch," Maggie said as she positioned Fern in a kitchen chair and tied a leopard-print apron cape around her neck. "She never laughs at my jokes," Maggie added for Fern's benefit.

Gretchen returned to her phone and pulled a bag of popcorn from the microwave. They were taking over, and Fern was glad of it. She felt like she was about to slip right back into her rotten old ways, but Maggie said she was not allowed.

"I can at least distract you from your misery. But hopefully, with the help of a good, old-fashioned, salon session, I can counsel you in the direction of your true dreams."

Fern nodded lamely. "Baby It's Cold Outside," jingled from Maggie's phone on the counter, and Fern wanted to slap it to the floor.

She sighed, instead. "My dream is to go to bed, snuggle with my cat, and wake up on December 26."

"Well, that's not an option. He said he wanted to talk, right?" Maggie pressed.

Fern nodded while Maggie—whose roots were darker than ever and whose face was washed out behind her fading freckles—painted strands of Fern's limp hair and folded them up into the neatly cut squares of aluminum.

"He felt tricked. Like he showed up, and I seduced him but all the while I wanted a divorce."

"I thought *he* wanted a divorce," Gretchen chimed in.

Maggie glared at her daughter. Fern allowed herself a small smile. "Are you your mother's assistant?" Fern asked.

"Apprentice," Maggie replied, her face aglow with pride. "She's in esthetician school."

Fern complimented the duo. Toffee pranced into the kitchen to assess the intruders. Gretchen bent over to offer pets and soon enough the two had settled into the chair opposite.

"Do you love him?" Gretchen asked, stowing her phone face down on the tabletop.

Fern frowned at the teenager who, thanks to her mother, was clearly up to speed on Fern's private drama.

"What do you mean?" Fern asked.

"Do you love this guy? Or do you love the idea of this guy?" Gretchen asked again.

Fern thought about it. "What do you mean 'the idea' of him?"

Maggie slapped on more dye and answered for her daughter. "Gretchen is of the generation where people post about things. They post that they are dating or hooking up or whatever. Whether or not they are *actually engaging* in said activities is another matter," she said, laughing. "Gretchen has been dating Gary-the-realtor's kid for two years," she went on.

"Mama," Gretchen whined holding her hands up in an outcry.

"Oh, hush up. You know Fern's business. She's got a right to yours now. That's how womanhood works, young lady."

Gretchen sank back into her seat and rolled her eyes.

Maggie continued. "Gretchen loves the *idea* of Jake. He's a Hickory Grove boy. His dad has a little money. It's easy stuff. But Gretchen doesn't love him. She ain't *in* love with him." Maggie slipped into bad grammar, but Fern ignored it and smiled at the little secret.

"So why don't you break up with him?" Fern asked gently.

Gretchen shook her head. "It's too hard. Easier just to leave things alone, you know? Not rock the boat. It's fine, anyway."

Fern nodded. Easier for her would be to leave things alone, too. She liked the idea of that. But she loved Stedman. There was no question. He would make her life harder, and she was scared to complicate her recently stabilizing reputation among the local community.

But maybe he was worth it. Maybe, this time, he was worth fighting for. Maybe they needed a break, and then needed to two-step a little to find their groove again. Stranger things had happened. That was for sure.

***

"Voila," Maggie announced, as she held a mirror in front of Fern's freshly blown-out hair.

It was the next morning. The morning of the tree lighting ceremony.

Maggie had declared that a good makeover didn't occur in one sitting. Plus, she wanted Fern to look perfect for the event, anyway.

The night before, the girls had stayed up late, talking about love and life. Fern invited them to stay for a Christmas movie, but they had declined. Becky didn't want to babysit all night, anyway.

The loneliness had crept in, and Fern considered calling Stedman.

But she carried a little anger, still. Anger she may not overcome. He jumped to conclusions just like she had. Neither one had learned how to give the other a chance to explain himself or herself. Their communication was as advanced as Gretchen and Jake's. Pitiful, really.

Just as they promised, Liesl and Trish had turned up with the finishing touches.

The women returned again at five o'clock, bringing their baked contributions. In the meantime, they were slated to speak on the air live with WFEA FM Christian Talk Radio to discuss the event and advertise as much as possible in as short a time frame as possible.

Along with them, the Hickory Grove High School Choir was due to arrive and begin warming up for a lineup of Christmas carols. Fern was starting to wonder if this little tree lighting ceremony was taking a new direction. Never before had they hosted a choir or gone on air to advertise.

And so that's why Maggie decided to add in a blow dry, makeup, and styling. Or so she claimed. Maggie was the type to harbor ulterior motives, after all.

Fern took the mirror from Maggie and peered carefully at herself. She was relieved to see that beneath the blonde, swooping waves and behind the heavier eye makeup, she was still Fern Monroe. Fern Gale. Something in the middle, maybe.

Actually, she looked to be very much like her old self. The one who went to college and worked in a museum in Louisville and fell in love with Stedman Gale.

Then again, just yesterday he said he was still in love with her. He kissed her despite her dull hair and sallow complexion. And he kissed her hard. This makeover wasn't to lure Stedman back into her arms. She'd already done that without even trying.

This makeover was a reminder. A refresher.

Stedman had said it himself, she *had* changed. And though her whirlwind change was, by and large, for her own good, she couldn't lose sight of who she was. A woman with a quiet life who enjoyed watching movies.

So, then, who was Stedman?

Well, very likely, he was her ex-husband. Or, he would be soon.

Chapter 25: 2014

GoneWithTheGale has entered the chat.

MiracleOnPineTreeLn: You're here.

GoneWithTheGale: For you? Always. How was work? Are we still meeting for lunch tomorrow? Would dinner be better? Dinner would be better for me.

MiracleOnPineTreeLn: Stedman...

GoneWithTheGale: ...Fern?

MiracleOnPineTreeLn: I really like you, Stedman.

GoneWithTheGale: Because we're soul mates. I know. I really like you, too, Fern. I think that's clear.

MiracleOnPineTreeLn: Stedman, where do you think this is going?

GoneWithTheGale: Wherever love usually goes...

MiracleOnPineTreeLn: Love??? That's... a strong word.

GoneWithTheGale: We've dated for like eight months. I feel well within my rights, here.

MiracleOnPineTreeLn: True. Okay, then. In that case, tell me: where does "love usually go?"

GoneWithTheGale: Well, if it's true love, then it goes the distance.

MiracleOnPineTreeLn: True love, huh?

GoneWithTheGale: Has to be true.

MiracleOnPineTreeLn: How do you know if you TRULY love someone?

GoneWithTheGale: Oh, there are lots of clues.

MiracleOnPineTreeLn: Go on...

GoneWithTheGale: You respect the person.

MiracleOnPineTreeLn: Sure, of course.

GoneWithTheGale: You worry about them! You worry about if they are safe and happy. You worry about the things they care about or worry about, too.

MiracleOnPineTreeLn: Good point.

GoneWithTheGale: And, you think about the person a lot. Sometimes maybe those thoughts aren't nice, but the person is still on your mind.

MiracleOnPineTreeLn: Bad thoughts??

GoneWithTheGale: Well, yeah. You're angry with them or mad at them or disappointed in them. Maybe they are mad at you. Or just sad. And you think about that. Even if you don't know what to say.

MiracleOnPineTreeLn: Hmm. I get it, I suppose.

GoneWithTheGale: But, see, Fern, TRUE LOVE means you go back to them even after the fight or after your disappointment or after their anger. You always go back if you truly love them.

MiracleOnPineTreeLn: Well what if the fight is really bad? Isn't there a... line?

GoneWithTheGale: If you truly love someone, and you miss them, and that person is your soul mate, then you don't have a choice.

MiracleOnPineTreeLn: Hey, now. There are always a couple of choices.

GoneWithTheGale: If you are committed to each other, then the choice begins much earlier on, though. Way before a fight can derail anything.

MiracleOnPineTreeLn: When does the choice begin?

GoneWithTheGale: For you, specifically, it is going to happen very soon.

MiracleOnPineTreeLn is typing...

GoneWithTheGale: By the way, how about that dinner tomorrow? I have a question...

Chapter 26

One last glance in the foyer mirror to check that her lipstick hadn't slid onto her teeth and Fern was ready.

She'd done everything she could to do for the night to be perfect. The rest was up to God.

Liesl, Trish, Annie, and the rest of the Ladies Auxiliary huddled together at not one, but *four* red-draped tables in the driveway. Baked goods and paper products covered every inch. Liesl's uncle, Gary Hart of Hickory Grove Realty, had brought and set up an oversized tent to cover the tables as snow fell on the gathering crowds.

It was a light, sparse snow, and if you weren't holding a cup of hot cocoa or a plate of chocolate chip cookies, you might not even realize it was snowing.

The choir had finished their rehearsal in the garage and was now filling a squat set of bleachers brought in by Zack Durbin from Hickory Grove Unified School District's facilities department. The radio station was in attendance, camping out in the garage with their equipment and playing Christmas tunes until the choir started and would do so during breaks.

Locals had begun to show up, first stopping off at the tables to get their warm treats and then lingering in little groups around the tree.

By six o'clock, the sun had begun to set. Gary Hart and his brother, Rich, turned on the heater lamps.

Fern's house was aglow with clear globes on the outside. She lit the upstairs bedroom, the parlor, and the great room from within, which added a lace backdrop to the pretty white lights.

Slowly, as more and more people trickled up Pine Tree Lane from Main Street, and the property grew dense with cheerful onlookers, the snowfall fell away, leaving behind a light drapery—just enough of a covering to act like a pretty duvet on a neatly made bed.

Fern stood on her front porch and leaned into the garland-spiraled railing as she watched for familiar faces. Though she was proud to host such a spectacle, she much preferred to watch rather than partake.

Becky showed up on the arm of her boyfriend. Together, they sipped hot cocoa and nibbled on cookies, laughing into each other's necks and settling into a pair of Adirondack chairs that was tucked away from the crowds.

Maggie had indicated she might be a little late to the event. It came as a last-minute text. Trouble in paradise, it seemed. Then again, was Maggie's life ever a paradise?

The lighting ceremony would commence at seven o'clock. At six forty-five, she and all four of her children waddled over from the up the street. No Travis in sight. No surprise.

At exactly seven, the event M.C., Liesl, of course, took the D.J.'s microphone and shepherded the two-hundred or so attendants toward the centerpiece, Eleanor Monroe's fourteen-foot-tall artificial Christmas tree, decked to the nines in ornaments and glittery ribbons of tinsel. An antique tree topper—an angel—loomed high on the top, watching down over the celebration.

Fern scanned the crowd. Disappointed, she sank into a chair on her deck.

"Welcome to the Hickory Grove Township Annual Tree Lighting Ceremony!" Liesl cheered into the mic as the crowd padded their mittened palms together with her. A few errant whistles came from the far corners of the property.

As Liesl went on, it seemed at least fifty others had joined in the growing circle around the tree.

"This year, we are delighted and grateful to host our ceremony here, at the home of Fern Gale, one of Hickory Grove's finest."

Fern blushed beneath her knit cap on the porch as people looked curiously up at her. She realized her position away from them drew more attention than she intended.

She nodded as everyone clapped vaguely in her direction. She could hear Maggie's whooping cheer for her from the hot cocoa station.

"And now, without further ado, on behalf of the Little Flock Catholic Ladies Auxiliary, I am honored to..." Liesl paused dramatically as the choir struck up an acoustic rendition of "O, Holy Night." But just before they broke into the lyrics, she dropped her voice low and, as if she were a classically trained radio star, Liesl cooed, "wish you good tidings from *The Christmas House*."

Fern took her cue and plugged in the extension cord beneath the front bay window. The crowd oohed over the scene. A gorgeously trimmed tree in fresh snow at one of the most beautiful homes in George County. A stately ancestral home.

But it was all sadly anticlimactic for Fern. As the choir carried on in their song and the crowd joined in, their voices lifting on cloudy breaths up to the heavens, Fern opened her front door and slipped inside her house.

All the change—all the cleanness and freshness—made her sadder than ever. Earlier, she'd locked Toffee into a little cat kennel in her bedroom. Now, it felt cruel and unusual. She stole away upstairs and unlocked the cage, plucking the little fluff out and murmuring apologies into her smooth coat as she descended the staircase and trudged to the great room.

Once there, she pulled the lace curtains closed and turned on the television set. She was happy the town found such pleasure in her old house. And she was happy to feel free to chase her dreams. Her collectibles could become inventory. Her house could become public property.

She opened her laptop and reread the last email she'd sent, checking for something.

For truth. For insight. For anything that would tell Fern *who she was*.

Dear GoneWithTheGale,

Remember when you proposed to me? We went out for dinner. I think you ordered the steak and didn't eat a single bite.

You asked me to choose you. And I did, of course.

I still do. I've been afraid of what I would say to you or what you would say to me. But I still choose you. And, remember? You chose me, too.

Stedman, please come home.

I miss you.

MiracleOnPineTreeLn

Fern swallowed a growing lump in her throat. She could have written so much. She *did* write so much. She documented how she changed and who she was. She documented everything she had learned about herself in two short weeks.

And she erased every last word. Because even though her house was clean and people were gathered outside her very front door, Fern never *really* changed.

She just became who she always was.

Toffee leapt from beside her and pranced across the floor toward the front hall. Fern panicked, thinking one of the guests was entering to use the restroom and might accidentally let Toffee out into the Christmas chaos.

But as her eyes followed the brown and white fur, they landed on a pair of boots that had stopped at the threshold between the great room and the foyer. A pair of rugged hands plucked Toffee up from the ground. Fern followed the cat's ascension.

He lifted Toffee up and, this time, did more than give her scratches behind the ears. He buried his face in Toffee's neck, kissing the cat shamelessly.

Fern met his gaze and smiled, tears in her eyes.

"She really loves me," Stedman said, pointing a finger up to the mistletoe that hung above Toffee and him.

Fern nodded, unable to talk.

"I got your email," Stedman went on, nearing her. "I know what you were afraid I'd say," he added.

Nervous, Fern frowned and stood from the sofa, backing away half a step. "Oh?"

"Yes," he answered, nodding gravely and stepping past her and to the hearth. "You were afraid I'd say you need to learn how to start a darn fire."

She laughed while he started to work on the partially charred log inside the hearth. The sounds of the evening acted as a pretty background for his surprise visit. Fern swallowed hard and stared at the back of Stedman. His flannel shirt and snow vest. Jeans stuffed into boots.

"Thank you for coming," she said, her voice low. "Do you want a drink or anything?"

Warmth spread immediately from the fireplace and he turned to reveal the log had caught. Its flamed lapped above the grate and he added a second smaller log for good measure. "Actually," he began to answer as he brushed his hands off on his jeans. "I want to know what the heck you were talking about." He moved his hands to his hips and faced her squarely, his face impassive, his body tense. "Fern, I came and helped you, and it changed things. And then more change happened. You with your friends and your tidy house. Those are great. Earlier I sort of suggested I didn't like them. But, I do. I guess, Fern—I guess I'm just not sure where to go with this." Stedman lifted his hands helplessly then dropped them back down. "The burst pipe, then dinner. It made me nervous. Excited, too." He allowed a small smile, but went on. "I don't know. I had no idea why you'd draw up divorce papers when it seemed like things were moving toward a reunion. That's all. I'm confused."

Fern closed her eyes briefly then opened them. "I was confused, too. When you left four years ago, I fell apart. I quit my job, Stedman. The only two people I had—well I didn't have them anymore." Her chin dropped to her chest.

She felt his arms wrap her as he buried his face in her neck. "I'm sorry, Fern. I'm sorry."

Pushing back, Fern held a finger to his lips. "Stedman, it's all right. Really, it is. And anyway, I..."

He cocked his head and stared at her, waiting.

"Stedman," she began. "For too long, I was a daughter and not a wife. I can admit that. I am sorry for it, too. But Stedman," Fern gripped his face between her hands as her husband wrapped his arms around her waist.

"Yes?" he whispered.

"I love you. I miss you. And..."

He nuzzled her neck again, kissing the edge of Fern's jaw as she smiled and pushed him away again.

"And...?" he asked, his gaze heavy with love.

"And *you* have a choice to make," Fern answered, simply. A smile danced across her lips.

Stedman knitted his eyebrows together and rubbed his hands up her arms before bringing her face to his in a deep, slow kiss.

Moments later, they parted, and Stedman went on. "I choose you, Fern. I chose you years ago, and I choose you again. I never *didn't* choose you," he said, but she held her finger to his lips.

"I know, I know. I didn't mean that," Fern said, shaking her head.

"Then what did you mean? What choice?"

Fern's face fell serious as she held up the television remote and answered him, "You have to choose right now. *Home Alone* or *A Christmas Story*?"

Stedman laughed and pulled Fern close to his chest. "Actually," he answered, tugging her toward the bay window to look out at the front property of *The Christmas House,* aglow with lights and people and holiday cheer. "How about *Miracle on Pine Tree Lane*?"

Epilogue

"I have to be honest, Fern," Maggie said over two steaming mugs of coffee. It was the day after Christmas. Stedman was still upstairs in bed. Maggie's kids would sleep for another hour or two.

The women were creating a game plan for their post-Christmas bargain hunting trip. Becky Linden was joining, too.

"Okay?" Fern asked, running her hand down Toffee's back.

"Why an antique shop?"

Fern frowned, and the cat jumped off her lap and pranced away, refusing to defend her owner.

Maggie pressed on. "Why don't you just go back to the museum and work there?"

Fern thought for a moment before replying. "Maggie, I have this huge house. It deserves more than just Stedman and me. And Toffee. It deserves *something*. I have pieces—products—on hand. I know the pieces well. I can sell antiques. And I can honor my mother and father here. And make use of this space. I won't feel guilty anymore. Not if I can do something more with it."

"Actually, that makes sense," Maggie answered, her expression unreadable. "Do you think you'll host more events here? Other than selling antiques? You know, like the tree lighting?"

"Absolutely. I've already talked to the Ladies Auxiliary about a New Year's Eve party. And Zack Durbin over at Hickory Grove Unified wants to rent the front lawn for a fundraising gala. It's incredible, really. I went from the nuthouse to the community center."

"Do you like that?" Maggie asked.

Fern shrugged. "I love that people want to be here. I don't have to do much. I can sort of just be around. Make things look pretty. And watch from the sidelines. Really, it's perfect." Fern smiled at Maggie and sipped from her mug.

A sadness shadowed the redhead's face.

Fern frowned. "Everything okay, Maggie?"

Everything did *not* seem okay. Deep auburn roots were creeping down her longish, unbrushed tresses. Though pretty without makeup, a sallow complexion had set in on Maggie's delicate face, drawing her mouth down toward premature jowls.

Maggie shook her head. "Yes and no, Fern. I'm happy for you. I see you chasing your dreams and everything falling into place. I'm happy for you."

Fern felt herself flush. "You've been a great friend to me, Maggie. It's my turn to help you. What can I do?"

"No, no. I don't need handouts. I'm just fine. *We're* just fine," she assured.

"The kids seem happy?" It came out like a question, and Fern swallowed her discomfort.

"The kids are clueless. And that's just how I want them to be." Tears pricked Maggie's eyes and she brushed them away with the back of her hand.

Fern clicked her tongue. "Aw, Maggie. Come here," she said, standing and wrapping the frail mother in a hug.

"I just hate him so much," Maggie sobbed.

Fern thought about Stedman's notions of true love and wondered if Maggie and Travis ever had that. She asked as much.

"No," Maggie answered. "I don't think I ever loved him, Fern. It was a high school thing that lasted too long."

Fern's eyebrows rose. She didn't know the history between Maggie and her husband. This was all news to her. "Why did you stick it out?"

"For the kids. And I always will stick it out for them. I'll do whatever it takes to keep them safe and happy."

"Even if that means *you* aren't?"

"Oh, Fern. Travis would never touch a hair on my head. I'm safe, trust me. A little danger might even do our marriage good. Who knows?" Maggie's eyes dried and she let out a laugh. "Well, that's not true. Nothing can save our marriage. Not even a thrill."

"But what if you aren't happy, Maggie?"

"Just because I'm not happy with Travis doesn't mean I'm not happy with life."

Fern shook her head. "Haven't you considered leaving him?"

"Fern, I don't believe in divorce. And anyway, where would I take the kids? We have a beautiful house next door. *Where would we go*?"

***

Learn more about the place Maggie calls home in *The Farmhouse*, the next book in the Hickory Grove series.

Other Titles by Elizabeth Bromke

Hickory Grove:
The Schoolhouse
The Farmhouse
The Innkeeper's House
The Quilting House, A Hickory Grove Christmas
Birch Harbor:
House on the Harbor
Lighthouse on the Lake
Fireflies in the Field
Cottage by the Creek
Bells on the Bay
Gull's Landing:
The Summer Society
The Garden Guild
The Country Club
Indigo Bay:
Sweet Mistletoe

Acknowledgments

The more books I write, the more people I meet. I've so enjoyed getting to know my readers and other authors in the romance and women's fiction communities. *The Christmas House* has brought to my attention just how crucial my relationships with readers and writers really are.

Thank you to my writing sorority, including Mel McClone, Laura Burton, Marika Ray, Daria White, Dawn Malone, DeAnn Grady, Gigi Blume, IreAnne Chambers, Kayla Eshbaugh, Rachael Bloome, Wendy May Andrews, and Emily Clark. Of course, Dave Cenker, too! Recently, I worked with Mandi Blake and Christina Butrum. A huge thanks to you two for your eyes on this book. Of course, thanks to Krissy Moran for being a fabulous and encouraging editor!

Judy Peterson was a force within this story—pushing Fern to the limits of her personhood (or characterhood, as the case may be). Without your guidance and encouragement, Judy, Fern's story might have been stuck in a reality television episode. Thank God for you!

Thank you to my mother and aunt for letting me talk and talk and talk about Fern and Stedman. You've listened to it for so long now. Look how far we've come! Grandma and Grandbob—thank you for Little Flock and Hickory Grove. What a town.

Grandma E., thank you for unwittingly inspiring an important part of this story: Fern's tragedy: Eleanor Monroe's Christmastime passing. This one is for you and your very own mother, Alvina Zick, who passed on Christmas Day.

Ed and Eddie, always for you.

About the Author

Elizabeth Bromke is the author of the Maplewood series, Hickory Grove series, and Birch Harbor series. In her writing, Bromkes weaves the triumphs and trials of modern relationships. Her settings are rural and notalgic, lending themselves beautifully as backdrops to emotional, heartwarming stories.

In her free time, Elizabeth enjoys reading, walking, and spending time with family. Learn more at elizabethbromke.com today.

CPSIA information can be obtained
at www.ICGtesting.com
Printed in the USA
BVHW041802021121
620550BV00007B/452